TORCHED
BURNT BY A GASLIGHTER

—

A Novel by Deborah A. Griffiths

TORCHED
BURNT BY A GASLIGHTER

—

A Novel by Deborah A. Griffiths

Printed and Electronic Versions
ISBN: 978-1-956353-36-5
ISBN eBook: 978-1-956353-37-2
(Deborah A. Griffiths/Motivation Champs)

The book was printed
in the United States of America.

To order additional copies or bulk order contact the publisher,
Motivation Champs Publishing. www.motivationchamps.com

I dedicate this to Jeffrey, Larry, and Megan

I will always love you!

And to my Lord, Jesus Christ

Thank you for always guiding, protecting, and loving me!

CONTENTS

FOREWORD
By Glenn Sinkule

My wife, Claudia, and I, are the Co-Founders of The Nicole Sinkule Foundation. I've known Debbie Griffiths, the author of this book, for many years. We met and formed our relationship at Biola University.

Through our studies, we got to know each other well through our exam preparations and general Biblical discussions. I was dealing with prostate cancer at the time, and Debbie always lent a hand. Little did I know of the challenges she was facing.

In 2005, my 25-year-old daughter, Nicole, was brutally murdered. Asleep in her bed, her boyfriend came to her, used a claw portion of the hammer to tear her skull apart, and then left the hammer in her head.

I tell you this to point out the gaslighting she endured before her murder. I call it emotional abuse.

The murderer kept telling her that she wasn't anything without him, that she was worthless, and put her down at every junction to manipulate her mind. Finally, he lied to her and seduced her mind. She was so in love with him that she followed along, thinking she would change him.

My daughter, Nicole, journaled the following: "I'm stuck between reality and a dream-Nicole Crystal Sinkule (NCS)." Her murderer manipulated her mind saying what she heard, and saw wasn't real. He told her it was just a joke; she was too sensitive and that it never happened", leaving Nicole to write in her journal, "If only I acted in a different way" (NCS), causing her to question her own mind.

This novel explains gaslighting and provides a scenario of a person gaslighted. It's easy to read, gives excellent knowledge into the signs of gaslighting abuse, and highlights the RED Flags one should be familiar with to avoid these situations.

Gaslighting is one of many cases of abuse to become aware of, "Become Aware and Share," just as Debbie has done with this book.

If you, or anyone you know, might be being abused, please get in touch with Domestic Violence Hotline 800-799-SAFE (7233).

PREFACE

What is Gaslighting? Merriam-Webster defines gaslighting as the "psychological manipulation of a person usually over an extended period that causes the victim to question the validity of their thoughts, perception of reality, or memories and typically leads to confusion, loss of confidence and self-esteem, uncertainty of one's emotional or mental stability, and a dependency on the perpetrator."[1] The term "gaslighting" comes from the 1944 George Cukor film, *Gaslight*, starring Ingrid Bergman and Charles Boyer, where the man (Boyer) tries to convince his wife (Bergman) that she is going insane by dimming the gas lights and telling her that it is her imagination. As a result, she begins to doubt herself and her reality.

According to recent estimates, "more than 43 million women and 38 million men will experience mental or emotional abuse by an intimate partner, according to the Centers for Disease Control and Prevention."[2] Victims are from all walks of life – race, creed, and color. It knows no boundaries. As you read this, you, a family member, a friend, or a co-worker may be experiencing this form of domestic abuse. Know the signs and seek help if you or someone you know is a victim. You can find resources at the end of this book. But, for now, here are ten signs of gaslighting, according to the Newport Institute:

1. Lying about or denying something and refusing to admit the lie even when you show the proof.

2. Insisting that an event or behavior you witnessed never happened and that you remember it wrong.

---

1   "Gaslighting," *Merriam-Webster.com Dictionary*, Merriam-Webster, https://www.merriam-webster.com/dictionary/gaslighting. Accessed 13 June. 2022

2   "#TakeAStand Against Domestic Violence," Centers for Disease Control and Prevention, https://www.cdc.gov/injury/features/intimate-partner-violence. Accessed 21 June. 2022

3. Spreading rumors and gossip about you or telling you that other people are gossiping about you.

4. Changing the subject or refusing to listen when confronted about a lie or other gaslighting behavior.

5. Telling you that you're overreacting when you call them out.

6. Blame shifting in relationships – saying that if you acted differently, they wouldn't treat you like this, so it's really your fault.

7. Trying to smooth things over with loving words that don't match their actions.

8. Twisting a story to minimize their abusive behavior.

9. Minimizing their hurtful behaviors or words by saying something like, 'It was just a joke' or 'You're way too sensitive.'

10. Separating you from friends and family who might recognize your gaslighting abuse systems.[3]

This novel fictionalizes actual events to show the impact gaslighting has on its victims. Any identifying characteristics, such as names and locations, were changed to protect the privacy of those depicted. Gaslighting victims should seek professional help as it is available for those who contemplate leaving an abusive relationship, healing from such abuse, and learning to rebuild their lives in a healthy, productive manner. Many victims, such as Martha, characterized in this novel, have successfully rebuilt their lives.

---

3   *"How to Tell If Someone Is Gaslighting You,"* Newport Institute, https://www.newportinstitute.com/resources/mental-health/what_is_gaslighting_abuse. Accessed 13 June. 2022

CHAPTER 1

IF WORDS COULD KILL

"You will never make it, and no one will ever love you," Sam screamed at the top of his voice for the whole neighborhood to hear. With a reddened face and furrowed brows, his deep brown eyes glared at her. Martha was leaving their seventeen-and-a-half-year marriage marred with domestic abuse. Sam was well aware that Martha had asked for the divorce and had made plans to move to a new apartment. Sam could not stand the thought of sustaining a bruised ego for a failed marriage, but she had had enough. This marriage almost cost her life, not once but twice. She clenched her teeth and stared into his eyes as he yelled these words. Martha felt her blood pressure rise, but she was determined not to flinch and let him have any more control over her. *Martha wanted to say something but did not.* Instead, she thought, these are the wrong words to say to me, and I'm going to prove you wrong. She acknowledged that these words would drive her to succeed in building a better life for her and the kids. And she was determined to do just that. Nothing would stand in her way!

Slam! The door closed in Martha's face. She turned around to see a large make-shift box sitting in the driveway, approximately 8 feet high and wide. Sam had taken several boxes and hastily taped them together with brown packing tape to form one large, flimsy box. The box contained the belongings he allowed her to take from the home that he felt she needed for the kids. Martha had no idea what the items were that Sam stuffed into that box as he had not consulted her. The box was too big to fit in Martha's car and she had a hard time understanding why he created such a huge box that could not be lifted or transported. She thought that he could have easily packed the items into the smaller boxes.

Sam refused to let her back into the house to get the remainder of the items that were hers per the marital property agreement, including a rifle passed down from Martha's grandfather and a vintage 1965 Beatles album. Martha used her house key to get back into the home but noticed Sam changed the locks so she could not re-enter. Martha had been making trips back and forth to her new apartment and it was during this most recent trip that Sam changed the locks unbeknownst to her.

Martha called the police, who came about thirty minutes later. They told her there was nothing they could do. "So much for the 'good ole boy,' South," Martha muttered to herself. She tore open the box in the driveway to see what was in it. Most items were large toys that would not fit in the new apartment, but there were not any kids' clothes included in those belongings. Now she understood why Sam made his own version of a box. The items he thought the kids needed did not fulfill the basic needs of housing, clothing or food. She went through what was there, took what she could that would fit in the car, and left the remaining items in the driveway for all the neighbors to see. She drove away with the kids to begin a new life.

—

Years later, Martha reflected on those moments with her daughter. "Hard to believe that happened forty years ago, Mom," Rachel stated.

"Look how far we have all come since those days," Martha replied.

Rachel was the youngest of Martha's three kids. She was about four when the divorce happened but still had some lingering memories of the events, and her easy-going demeanor made it possible for her to heal faster than her two older brothers.

Today, the family was celebrating Martha, who was turning seventy-five. *"Seventy-five years! Where did the time go?* Martha pondered. It felt like yesterday when all her kids were small, and she was busy with carpools and PTA. Those years went by too fast, and she finds herself now retired and living with her daughter and her family. Life was good! Despite some challenges, Martha considered herself very blessed with a great family and great friends, and most of all, she was incredibly grateful for the love and protection God has shown her throughout the years.

The following day, Martha sat on the front porch watching the sun rise, casting a reddish glow on the western mountains. The temperature on the desert floor was rising, indicating it would be a triple-digit day. Martha reflected on her recent birthday celebration. Her thoughts turned as she began to meditate on her remaining years, wanting them to be purposeful.

Martha was still attractive for being seventy-five. However, her dishwater blonde hair was now beginning to show some gray. She was of average height and weight and kept active by watching her youngest grandchild, Sydney, who was four. She also enjoyed walking several miles a week and, when time permitted, she would play golf. Her fair skin showed some aging, but most people believe her to be ten years younger than she was. Martha had a quiet disposition, but her bright blue eyes twinkled, showing off her fun side.

Pitter-patter. Pitter-patter. Little feet ran down the hall. It was clear that one of the grandkids was up. "Grandma, what's for breakfast?" asked ten-year-old Sarah who opened the door to Martha's room.

"How about some pancakes?" replied Martha. Sarah shook her head yes. Martha got up and went to the kitchen to start breakfast. Sarah was the oldest of Rachel's children. She was tall for her age, and her long, dark brown hair showed off her hazel eyes.

Martha began preparing the pancake batter. Rachel was waking up Sydney, and James was busy helping six-year-old Michael, an exact carbon copy of his father, brush his teeth. Yes, the new day was here. Rachel, James, Michael, and Sydney came running downstairs to smell freshly cooked pancakes with maple syrup and sat at the table to eat. Finally, it was about time for the school bus to arrive for Sarah and Michael. Rachel quickly ate her breakfast and began packing their lunches. Before you know it, the school bus, blowing its horn, interrupted the morning's noise and commotion. Sarah and Michael were off to school. Soon after that, Rachel and James took off to work at their respective jobs – Rachel worked in Human Resources while James worked in construction. They both made a decent living, affording them the opportunity for a five-bedroom, two-story home with a nice-sized yard in a great neighborhood with good schools.

James and Rachel met about fifteen years ago at a relative's wedding. What started as a friendship soon turned into love, and they married a year later. James came from an upper-middle-class family that did well in the construction industry. He was a bit older than Rachel, but the age difference works in their favor. In addition, James was quite handsome with an average build, dark hair, and deep blue eyes. It was easy to see why Rachel fell in love with him.

It was just Martha and Sydney for the next few hours. Martha finished cleaning the kitchen while Sydney played with her toys in the family room. Martha completed dressing herself and Sydney, then turned and asked if she would like to go to the park. Sydney looked up at Martha with a beautiful, wide grin as if to say *yes*. They took off to the local neighborhood park.

Seeing the belt swing in the distance, Sydney immediately ran to the blue one and tried to climb on. Martha put her bag down on the wooden bench, helped Sydney onto the swing, and began to push her. Sydney was giggling with excitement but soon tired and headed for the sandbox. Once there, Martha put sunblock and a hat on her to protect her from the sun. Another little girl soon joined her, and they began building sandcastles. Martha smiled at the two little girls and prayed that their lives would always be this carefree. Unfortunately, she knew it might not because her life had been full of challenges, heartbreak, and pain.

Sydney shouted out, "Grandma, I'm getting hungry." Martha gave her some water and a small snack of crackers from the bag, but that did not satisfy her. So, they headed home. Martha made lunch, and they ate outside on the patio. After lunch, she cleaned up and put Sydney down for her nap. Martha appreciated the fact that she had about an hour's break before Sydney would awaken.

Downstairs, Martha went to turn on the television, but decided she did not want to watch anything. Instead, she preferred to sit in silence. Yesterday's birthday celebration deeply impacted her, and she began to reflect on her life.

CHAPTER 2

IN THE BEGINNING

Martha was born on September 11th in Santa Monica, California. Her parents, Paul and Donna, had been married three years and already owned their first home before Martha came along. Three years later, Martha's sister, Mary, was born. Around this time, Martha's parents started a painting company where, in the beginning, her dad painted houses. The company grew to a formidable size, and soon, they were painting large commercial buildings, including museums and hospitals. The business flourished and provided the family with a comfortable lifestyle. Paul managed all the bidding and oversight of the crews while Donna did the payroll and the books. They were a good team.

This business arrangement allowed Martha's mother to work from home while raising Martha and Mary. Martha recalled many times when her mother served as the Classroom Mom and helped at the school's monthly Hamburger and Hot Dog days. As the business grew, Donna went into the office part-time to do the books, but she always cleaned the house, cooked meals, and ensured Martha and Mary went to school. Looking back, Martha acknowledged that her mom was one of the original Super Moms before it came into fashion. In those days, the norm was for women to stay at home. Nowadays, women hold full-time jobs while raising kids.

Martha's dad was busy growing the business but was always home by 5:00 pm for dinner. Friday nights were notable as they all went to dinner at a local restaurant. The restaurants were not fancy, but this was a time to celebrate a successful week and each other on the week's accomplishments. Martha's favorite memory was when her dad took her and her sister to school, especially on rainy days. They always joked that they preferred their dad take them to school as he got them there faster. Their mom was a bit of a slowpoke and extremely cautious when driving. She learned to drive later in life and never enjoyed the process, but she never got a ticket or had an accident.

The best part of growing up was the annual vacations. Because of the stress of running a business and never knowing when there might be enough of a break between jobs to get away, some vacation destinations were last-minute and unplanned- always the adventure! Some memorable trips included Yellowstone National Park, Yosemite, Sequoia, Hawaii (a couple of times), and a few trips back east to visit Paul's old Army friend and his family. One of the trips included driving from South Carolina to Washington D.C. Along the way, the family made two stops at George Washington's home at Mount Vernon and Thomas Jefferson's home, known as Monticello. It was a great trip.

But Martha's favorite trip happened when she was about twelve years old. The family went to a dude ranch in Colorado for a week. The mornings and afternoons entailed horseback riding along trails that highlighted the beauty of the Rocky Mountains. This beauty sharply contrasted with the Southern California postage stamp lots and concrete freeways she was used to. During that week, the family went on two side trips. One was to Mesa Verde National Park to see the cave dwellings, and the other was taking the last remaining single-gauge train to Silverton. The week ended with a mini rodeo on the ranch where everyone participated in fun and games. Martha's parents were not into horseback riding, so they opted for some jeep excursions to see the countryside. A couple of the ranch hands, who were around sixteen or seventeen, lingered around their cabin and gave Martha the eye as she appeared much older than twelve. She developed breasts and began her period at age eleven, much younger than the other girls her age. So, it was not unusual for teenage boys to stare at her, but her dad ensured the boys kept their distance when he was around. He was very protective of his girls!

—

Thud! Martha's attention turned to the sound coming from upstairs. "Uh oh," she muttered. "Somebody is up from their nap." Martha went upstairs to check on Sydney. Sure enough, she found Sydney standing on a chair she pulled into the closet. Sydney was busy pulling clothes off the hanger, which ended up on the floor, unaware that her grandma had caught her in the act.

Martha laughed and said, "Sydney, you are just like your mom. She did the same thing when she was little." Sydney turned around and delivered a big grin. It was the same sheepish grin that Rachel used to give at that age. Martha was amazed at how closely Sydney resembled Rachel – both had auburn hair and dark brown eyes. Martha continued, "Let's get off this chair, and I will help you pick something out." She lifted Sydney off the chair and selected a pair of blue shorts and a light blue tee shirt.

"Sydney," Martha quipped, "Let's hang up these clothes and start some laundry before your brother and sister get home from school."

"Okay, Grandma," Sydney replied and gave Martha her outfits, one at a time. Fifteen minutes later, they were done and headed to get the dirty clothes from the hamper.

Once the washer started, Sydney said, "Grandma, let's read some books."

"Okay, Sydney. Go pick out a couple of books, and we will do some reading." Sydney loved Dr. Seuss and soon found a book and brought it to Martha.

They went downstairs, sat on the couch, and began reading. Martha realized this was not the first time she had read this book to Sydney. No, it was more like the millionth time. Martha was sure Sydney had memorized the stories as she recited them as Martha read the words. Martha stopped mid-sentence, "Sydney, what is this word?"

"It's fish."

"That's correct, Sydney, very good." Martha did this a couple more times and saw that Sydney did recognize words.

Martha tightly hugged Sydney, "You are such a smart little girl, and I love you to pieces."

"I love you, too," replied Sydney.

After finishing the story, Martha and Sydney went upstairs to put the clothes into the dryer.

As they were coming down the stairs, the school bus squealed announcing its arrival in the neighborhood. The bus would be in front of their house in a couple of minutes, dropping off Sarah and Michael. Sydney was excited to see her siblings, and soon, Sarah and Michael walked through the door. The noise level at the front door went from zero to sixty in a split second.

The kids threw down their backpacks in the entry hall while everyone began talking. "How was your day? How did you do on the test? Do you have homework? What is for dinner?"

Martha did not know where to begin, so she told Sarah and Michael to take their backpacks upstairs, wash their hands, and come back for an afternoon snack.

"Come on, Sydney, please help me with the snacks and put them on the table," Martha said.

They went to the kitchen to prepare a quick snack for all of them. Sarah and Michael quickly returned downstairs, and the four enjoyed fruit, cheese, and a nice cold glass of water. Martha asked Sarah about her test and how she performed. Sarah responded that the test went well and thanked Martha for her help with studying.

Then, Michael piped in, "We started learning fractions today. It is a bit complicated."

"Really," replied Martha. "What's so hard about fractions?"

"Well, there's just too much simplifying for me."

Martha chuckled. "You mean finding the lowest common denominator?"

"Yeah, that's it," said Michael.

"It's not as hard as you think, but it helps to know your multiplication tables," Martha replied.

Michael just stared at her, like a deer in headlights, as math was not one of his favorite subjects.

Not wanting to feel left out, Sydney told everyone that she went to the park with Grandma, which made everyone smile.

Looking at the clock, Martha realized it was time to start dinner. Rachel and James were usually home by 5:30 pm, and she always liked to have their meals waiting for them. Martha recalled the days of being a single, working mother and how she always believed that it would be a nice treat to come home to a meal already prepared.

Martha told everyone to put their dishes in the kitchen and directed Sarah and Michael upstairs to begin homework. She looked at Sydney, "Come on upstairs and help me with the laundry." Sydney eagerly climbed the stairs.

"Boy, to have the energy of a child again," Martha muttered. With the laundry finished and put away, Sydney and Martha headed downstairs to start dinner. It was spaghetti in a meat sauce with a nice salad and garlic bread. Meal preparations began, and the two set the table together.

Rachel and James arrived home to the aroma of a tasty Italian meal, and happy children who were excited to see their parents. Martha smiled at all the excitement and then announced dinner would be ready in five minutes, so everybody should get ready to eat.

Everyone scrambled to clean up while Martha put the food on the table. With everyone seated, James led the family in prayer to thank God for the food they were about to eat, and the blessings received. And the dinner conversation began with everyone talking about their day. Martha sat back and observed it all. Rachel looked over at her mom and asked if she is okay because she was so quiet. Martha explained she likes watching all the interaction and was happy to see everyone enjoying their dinner.

Looking at James, Rachel told him she would clean up the dishes while he helped the kids with their homework. The kids cleaned the table, and James took them upstairs. Rachel went to the kitchen while Martha headed to the couch to work on crocheting an afghan. She turned on the evening news to see what was happening.

—

Martha began having flashbacks of when her grandmother taught her to do embroidery work and crochet. Her grandmother was left a widow when she was in her thirties, and singlehandedly raised three girls to adulthood, including putting them through parochial grammar school and high school. Unfortunately, her grandmother died too young, at age sixty-seven, having a heart attack at work. She never had the chance to retire nor enjoy her retirement years. Her biggest dream was to hold her future great-grandchildren in her arms and would always ask Martha when she could expect to see her not-yet-conceived great-grandchildren.

Martha had only been married six months at the time of her death and always imagined seeing the joy on her grandmother's face as each of her children were born. She always admired her grandmother's grit and determination and relied on this strength as she went through her own issues.

—

Rachel finished cleaning the kitchen and came down to sit by Martha. "Mom, you are so quiet. Everything okay?"

"Yes, all is good. Celebrating a milestone birthday has given me a reason to pause and reflect on my life."

"Mom," Rachel said hugging her mom, "you know you are my rock. I love you so much."

Martha smiled, "I know, and I love you too."

Martha kissed everyone goodnight and went to her room. She loved her room. It was large enough for a queen-sized bed, a dresser, two nightstands, a television, and a blue reading chair. She grabbed a book, sat in the chair, and began reading. Her mind wandered to earlier in the day when she was thinking about her childhood.

CHAPTER 3

THE SCHOOL YEARS

Growing up in the 1960s was a decade of change, especially for the Catholic church because of Vatican II. Baptized Catholics as infants, Martha, and her sister Mary, followed in their mother's steps. She was Catholic, coming from generations of Catholics who had immigrated in the 1800s from Europe. Her dad, however, was never brought up with any formal religious education despite being baptized Lutheran. His family never went to church. Her dad, as a non-Catholic, had promised to raise any children from the marriage as Catholic. He gladly complied. Years later, Martha recalled asking her dad why he did not attend church. He told her that attending church does not make one a good person. Instead, he believed that if one strived to follow the Ten Commandments, that sufficed. So, it was natural for Martha to ask a follow-up question on why she had to go to church. Not expecting that question, Martha's dad told her he wanted more for her and that having a good foundation in faith was important. Martha only recalled seeing her father in the church when she or her sister received one of the sacraments, or at Martha's wedding. The last time her dad was in church was for his funeral, where he received a Catholic Mass and burial in a mission cemetery.

Around the time Martha was ready to start first grade, the Mass changed from Latin to English, the priest now faced the parishioners during Mass, and women no longer needed to wear head coverings. In addition, many convents changed from the traditional habits that nuns commonly wore, to new, shorter-length versions. These were significant changes for the Church, and it took years for them to be implemented and accepted.

Martha started the first grade at a new parochial school. Right away, her teacher kept moving her closer and closer to the front of the class. Then one day, she took a note home addressed to her parents. Martha was scared and thought she was in trouble. The letter revealed that Martha was squinting in the classroom and suggested that her eyes get checked. Her parents took her to an optometrist where they learned Martha needed glasses. She inherited nearsightedness from her maternal line. At least wearing glasses allowed Martha to learn and excel in school.

Martha attended parochial grammar school from the first grade to the eighth grade. Like all parochial schools, religious studies were part of the curriculum. These studies included learning Church doctrine from the Baltimore Catechism and attending Mass weekly with the class. Martha always enjoyed these classes and learning more about God. This foundation in faith would later play a key role in her life.

While Martha did well in school, mostly earning A's, she had to work hard for them, spending many hours with her nose in the books. She did not have many friends due to her commitment to her studies. Many others in the class were distant, possibly because of her high grades. If they only appreciated how hard she had to work. Her parents had a strong work ethic and instilled in Martha and Mary that they should always give 110% in whatever they undertook. It paid off for Martha because, at the eighth-grade graduation, she walked away receiving the most awards; what a sense of accomplishment to see that her arduous work paid off.

—

Click! One of the bedroom doors closed, startling Martha who had dozed off a bit. She picked up her book and started to read where she last left off. Again, her mind shifted to reflecting on her high school years.

Martha smiled, remembering how she had to practically beg her dad to let her go to an all-girls Catholic high school. He believed her mother had been too sheltered going to an all-girls high school, and he did not want that for either of his girls. He rationalized going to public school would give her a more well-rounded experience.

On the other hand, Martha saw the benefits of smaller classes, better education, and the school's camaraderie. After her parents visited the school, they agreed that Martha could attend on the promise that she would attend school dances and sporting events that the school coordinated with the other all-boys high schools in the area. This decision was easy for Martha, and she eagerly accepted the agreement.

Just before the first day of her freshman year, Martha's mother received a call from Rebecca, a junior at the high school. Rebecca explained that the school had a program where they partnered a junior with a freshman to welcome them and help them feel like they belong before they even start school. This program, known as Big Sister-Little Sister, also entailed coming over early in the morning before she was awake to take her out for breakfast in her pajamas. Martha's parents approved of this adventure which took Martha totally by surprise. She couldn't believe that her mother woke her up, told her to go downstairs and meet a stranger who would take her to a restaurant in her pajamas with everyone staring? She was so embarrassed but had fun at the same time. However, Martha found Rebecca likable and was glad the adventure took place. Rebecca took her home after breakfast and gave her a small figurine that she still has.

A couple of weeks later, school started. It was a whole new reality – changing classrooms for each class, lockers, and meeting new people. Martha found these new opportunities exciting and scary! And, like grammar school, Martha plunged her nose into her studies. However, on several occasions, she was the victim of various practical jokes, including shaving cream in her locker and the disappearance of her schoolbooks.

Martha came off a bit too serious, so this was a way to lighten her up and make her feel like she belonged.

Her sophomore and junior years were uneventful. Religious studies also played a significant part in her high school training. These studies built upon the foundation she had already received in grammar school and would continue to play a vital role in her life.

Martha attended some school dances and football games and always managed to have a date to the homecoming dances and proms. Her life was good. The years went by quickly, and soon it was her senior year with all the privileges it entailed. Mary was now a freshman, and Martha enjoyed using her senior privilege to cut in line at the vending machine in front of her sister. *Nothing like a bit of sibling rivalry*, Martha thought.

When it was time for Martha to start applying for colleges, her dad was insistent that she only apply to local colleges. According to him, "There is no way you will be far from home." Unlike getting her way to attend the high school of her choice, Martha would not win this battle. It did leave a narrow selection of colleges for her to attend, but she applied, and a couple of colleges accepted her application.

It was time for her to focus on graduation. Martha walked away with several top awards. Winning them was exhilarating, and hearing her dad tell her how proud he was of her made her happy. Graduation day finally came, and all the girls, including Martha, wore white dresses and carried a bouquet of yellow roses. It was a day she would never forget.

—

"Good night, Grandma," said Sarah as she knocked on the door. Martha awakened again and told her goodnight. Then, realizing she was too tired to read more of her book, she climbed into bed and turned off the light.

CHAPTER 4

MEETING IN THE PARK

Creek! Martha's bedroom door opened and there stood Sarah in the doorway. Martha motioned for her to crawl into bed, and Sarah eagerly complied.

"What are you doing up so early," Martha asked rubbing the sleep from her eyes.

Sarah shrugged her shoulders, "I don't know."

"Well, what should we make this morning for breakfast, Sarah?"

"How about eggs and bacon?" replied Sarah.

"Sure thing. Let me get up and start breakfast while you get ready for school."

"Ok, Grandma. See you downstairs for breakfast."

Martha went downstairs to start breakfast. The aroma of bacon cooking permeated the house. Soon everyone was downstairs eating while Rachel packed their lunches. The school bus honked its shrilly horn as it entered the neighborhood, alerting them that it was time for Sarah and Michael to get to school. They bolted out the door, with James and Rachel soon following.

Martha looked at Sydney, "Well, kid, it's just you and me. How about going to the park again today?"

Sydney looks up at Martha, smiled exclaiming, "Yippee!"

Martha and Sydney arrived at the park, and just like yesterday, Martha put a hat on Sydney and coated her with sunblock. Sydney ran off to play on the slides and jungle gym. Martha sat down on the light brown wooden bench and watched her granddaughter play. Just then, a woman with two small kids sat next to Martha. The woman told her children to go and play and that she would be watching. Martha smiled at the woman and introduced herself. Sheepishly, the woman glanced at Martha and said her name was Liz.

"Nice to meet you, Liz," Martha said. Liz just smiled as Martha continued, "How old are your children, and what are their names?"

Liz responded, "Jess is two, and Amy is four."

"Nice," replied Martha. She continued, "Sydney is my granddaughter, and she is four."

Liz smiled in response. She was a stunning young woman, about Rachel's age, with light brown hair and green eyes. She was well dressed, wearing pressed designer jeans and a designer blouse, and carried a high-end designer handbag. Jess and Amy, nicely dressed as well, appeared to be wearing clothing from a higher-end department store.

While trying not to be judgmental, Martha believed the money spent on the kids' clothes should go towards saving for the future. 'Kids grow way too fast to spend a lot of money on clothes,' Martha concluded. She learned this from her knowledge of having to clothe her kids, and while always wanting them to look nice and presentable, she found a way to do so more frugally. 'To each their own,' Martha reasoned.

Liz's phone rang, and she answered it. Martha could hear Liz's response to questions asked by whom she gathered was Liz's husband. She observed Liz's body tense up and saw her bite inside her lip. Seeing this brought back some memories of her own abusive marriage.

Liz hung up the phone, and both women sat silently watching the children play. Trying to lighten the mood, Martha asked Liz if she lived nearby. Liz shook her head, fighting back the tears preventing her from speaking. A couple of minutes later, Liz regained her composure and stated that she could not seem to do anything right to please her husband. "Can I ask you a question?" Martha asked.

Liz stared at her and nodded yes.

Martha continued, "Does your stomach react when you see his name come up on the caller ID on the phone or when you hear the garage door open, and you know he is returning?"

"Why, yes!" Liz said, surprised and perplexed. "How do you know this?" Liz asked. "Listen to your gut." Not wanting to return to this part of her past, Martha told Liz it was time for Sydney and her to go home.

"Wait," asked Liz, "Why did you tell me to listen to my gut?"

"I left my husband many years ago due to abuse. I wished I had listened to my gut instinct sooner than I did."

Shocked, Liz responded, "I would love to hear more if you are willing to share it?"

Martha told her that she and Sydney were typically at the park around this same time daily unless there was inclement weather. Liz told her she would be back, and everyone said their goodbyes.

"Looks like you have a new friend, Grandma."

"Yes, it looks that way," responded Martha.

Soon they arrive home to get something to eat, do laundry, and wait for the others to return home for the day.

At the dinner table, Sydney blasted, "Grandma met a new friend today at the park." Everyone stared at Martha, who admitted she had met a young woman at the park about the same age as Rachel. Not wanting to say more, Martha looked down at her plate and finished eating.

After dinner, Rachel asked Martha about the meeting in the park. Martha, looking at Rachel, said, "Her name is Liz, and I suspect she is in an abusive marriage. It makes me feel sad for her and her kids."

"Mom," Rachel responded, "Be careful. I know this is a sensitive area for you."

"Yes, it is," replied Martha. Then, with dinner completed, dishes washed and put away, the kid's homework done, and everyone bathed for the night, Martha retreated to her room.

CHAPTER 5

THE COURTSHIP

The following day found the same routine as Martha was the first to arise and start breakfast. Lunches were packed, the bus picked up Sarah and Michael, and Rachel and James left for work. Sydney looked up at Martha, "Well, Grandma, can we go to the park this morning?"

Martha smiled, "Yes, we can! Let's finish getting dressed so we can get going."

Arriving at the park, Martha was surprised to see Liz already there with her kids. Sydney bolted for the jungle gym while Martha went to the beige wooden bench to sit next to Liz. "Good morning," Liz said to Martha.

"Good morning, Liz. Such a beautiful morning," replied Martha.

Turning to Martha, Liz asked, "Martha, if you are up to it, I would love to hear more. I found your comment interesting, and I'm curious as to why I have these feelings. Things are not right at home, and I do not like how my husband speaks to the children and me."

Martha took a deep breath and said, "Liz, I do not mind talking about this. What I went through happened a long time ago. Please understand that I am not a professional, and if you are in danger or have questions on this, you should contact a professional."

Liz acknowledged that she understood and said that while nothing physical had happened, she did not like how her husband spoke to them.

Martha told her that she understood. "I met my future husband, Sam, the first week in college. He had missed the first class and approached me from behind after the second class met and asked if I had notes from the first session. I turned around and was shocked to see this incredibly handsome guy asking me for notes. I remember stumbling for the words to respond. I told him I did and lent him my copy of the notes to review. With a big grin, he thanked me and then asked me my name, which I told him. Sam then explained that he needed the notes as he missed the first class because he was in a car accident. He was okay, but his 1977 Ford Pinto was not.

"After his explanation, we parted ways to go to our next class. Later that afternoon, Sam saw me walking to my class and ran to catch up with me. He ran across one of the lawns and yelled my name and said hello. I stopped dead in my tracks, surprised that he would run to catch up with me. Sam asked where I was going for class, so I told him. He told me his plans for the afternoon and then asked me for my phone number. I gave it to him.

"We both needed to get to our next classes, so we said goodbye. As I walked to class, I was shocked that a guy, a cute guy by the way, asked me for my phone number."

"Martha, you are an attractive woman. Why would you think that a guy would not ask you for your phone number to ask you out?" Liz interrupted.

Martha smiled. "The truth is that I did not have much dating know-how, and it always appeared that I somehow intimidated men. I have not been able to figure that one out."

Liz chuckled and urged Martha to continue.

"Well, let's see. Sam and I started to date. Simple dates like dinner and a movie. He then introduced me to his parents and his sister. His father,

Miles, was a retired Colonel from the Marines. Miles married Theresa when he was in France in the late 1950s. Theresa was a native Parisian and spoke fluent French. Sam was born in Paris soon after Miles and Theresa married. The family eventually moved to the South, where Miles stayed for the remainder of his military career. A couple of years after Sam was born, Theresa gave birth to Sam's sister. After Miles retired from the military, the family relocated to California. Sam had already finished high school and was waiting for the one-year residency requirement to enter a state university."

Sydney ran over to Martha, asking for something to drink. Martha reached into her bag and held the bottle of water for Sydney as she took some sips. Sydney ran back to the jungle gym, and Martha continued her story. "Time spent with Sam's family was good. Theresa always cooked up a storm, and, after dinner, the family would play card games. I enjoyed that time. I had such a feeling of warmth and security, which I acknowledged was missing. My parents focused on their business. Family meals occurred, but we scattered for our night activities once dinner was over. I focused on getting good grades and studied constantly. I can now look back and realize that I was missing some emotional connection that I started to find with Sam and his family. I admit that the connection was meaningful but now see that it was the beginning of the isolation that would eventually come."

This last comment took Liz by surprise. "What do you mean by isolation?" Liz asked.

Struggling for the right words, Martha responded, "I did not realize, until many years later, that Sam found ways to keep me from having relationships with my family and friends. Any time I tried to establish friendly relationships with neighbors or with other mothers who had kids the same age as mine, Sam would find a way to put them down and discourage me from talking with them."

Liz glanced at Martha, "Oh, I see."

Martha asked her if her explanation sufficed. Liz slowly shook her head affirmatively.

"Liz, by the way, you are nodding your head. I need to ask you a question. Are you experiencing some of what I just described," Martha inquired? Liz remained quiet.

Martha continued, "The other memory I have of dating Sam occurred while we were both taking college classes. We had morning classes and would arrive in the parking lot around 7:30 each morning. Sam would come to my car and sit in the front seat, where we would listen to music and talk. One day, we both arrived in the parking lot simultaneously, but Sam did not get out of his car. I do not recall what he was doing or pretending to do, but as it was time to get to class, I got out of my car, and Sam got out of his.

"Sam did not speak to me – no hello, no how are you, nothing. I tried to speak to him, and he ignored me. Later that day, Sam finally told me what was bothering him. He began to yell at me, telling me I was selfish and why it was that he always had to do the work to get out of his car to come to mine. He walked away when I tried to explain that I did not know that this bothered him and that he should have told me rather than shutting me out. I was speechless and confused as I did not know what the fuss was. At any rate, I bought a card to give to him the next morning in which I apologized for hurting his feelings. From then on, I went to his car to keep the peace.

"Years later, I found the cards that we had given each other. All the cards I gifted to him began with me apologizing for what I now realize were over trivial things. When I saw this, I threw out all those cards. I was angry that I allowed myself always to think I was at fault and responsible for his actions."

Liz could see Martha's blood pressure rise as she recounted these memories.

Changing the direction of the conversation, Liz asked if Martha goes to church. She was curious to learn more about Martha's upbringing and, if so, how her faith played into this courtship.

Martha replied, "Yes, I was brought up Catholic and basically taught to love others above ourselves. While I know now that we should love ourselves, the emphasis always seemed to be about loving others first. Your question brings up something else I just recalled. Sam was baptized and brought up as a Lutheran. He would quote the Bible left and right, and I was embarrassed. The only Bible verses we heard were from Mass. Our religious studies in grammar and high school entailed learning the Baltimore Catechism and doing acts of service. I do not recall attending Bible studies until much later. Because I believed Sam was more knowledgeable than me regarding the Bible, I somehow told myself that he was holier or better than me. I now know that this is not true. It is easy to see now that he would talk the talk but could not walk the walk. It left me feeling inferior and another reason for him to gain more control."

Not wanting to upset Martha anymore, Liz indicated she needed to go home and would be back the next day. Martha stared at her watch, saw the time, and agreed to pick up the conversation the next time they were both at the park.

Martha and Sydney returned home. That afternoon sped by quickly, with Sydney taking her nap and Martha doing a load of wash. Later, Sarah and Michael returned home from school, and Martha began preparing that night's dinner.

Everyone took their usual turns talking about their day at the dinner table. When it was Sydney's turn, she told everyone that Martha had seen her new friend again. Rachel and Martha exchange glances. Rachel wanted to ensure her mom was okay as she assumed her mom had relived some painful memories. Martha smiled at Rachel as if to say that all was good. A few hours later, Martha said good night, retreated to her room, and went to sleep.

CHAPTER 6

GETTING MARRIED

A few days passed before Martha took Sydney back to the park. The weather had turned cooler which was the excuse Martha needed to avoid the park. She was still processing the last conversation she had with Liz. While years have passed, she continuously gauges herself on moving forward from her past. Finally, feeling better, she took Sydney's hand and went to the park. Sydney immediately spotted Liz's kids and told them she missed them. All three kids headed for the jungle gym.

Martha sat down on the bench next to Liz. "I'm so glad to see you," Liz said. "I worried I might have scared you off."

"No," replied Martha. "I am tougher than that. I was avoiding the cooler weather." Both ladies sat in silence, watching the kids play. Then, turning to Liz, Martha asked her how things were going at home.

"About the same," Liz responded. "He will be going out of town tomorrow for a week. That will give me a chance to breathe," Liz continued.

"Oh, I see," Martha replied.

Wanting Martha to continue her story but not wanting to upset her, Liz asked how Sam proposed thinking that everyone has a great wedding day.

"Well, let's see," Martha replied. "We had been dating about a year, and Sam proposed towards the end of our first year in college. He did all the right things – he asked my parents for my hand in marriage, got down on one knee, and presented me with a beautiful diamond ring. While we had talked about marriage, I had no idea he was this close to proposing. I said 'yes' and we began to make wedding plans.

"I acknowledged the wedding was going to happen in the Catholic church. We met with the priest and set a date for June 1979 – a year away from the date we became engaged. I cannot remember exactly why this happened, but Sam resolved to move the date up to December 1978, which sent my parents into a tailspin as they were paying for the wedding. They were upset that Sam took it upon himself to change the plans without consulting them.

"And to make matters worse, Sam's parents began to involve themselves in the wedding plans. This plan change caused such an uproar that both families met at my parent's home to 'have it out.' I sat at the top of the stairs trying to listen to the discussions, which heated up several times. This argument was disheartening. With no resolution, both families just tolerated each other from then on."

Liz's son came running up, asking for something to drink and a few crackers. Martha and Liz sat there and enjoyed watching him tell them about his adventures at the jungle gym. Then, finally, finishing his crackers, he went back to play.

Martha continued, "One of my favorite memories is finding my wedding dress. My Mom and I went shopping, and we found the dress at the first store we entered. The dress was beautiful. It was an A-line style in ivory with capped sleeves. The train in the back of the dress was long, and the whole dress covered in lace and pearl beads. A matching floor-length veil was trimmed with lace all around the edge. I felt like a princess."

Liz caught Martha smiling as she was describing her dress. "Your dress sounds stunning."

Martha turned to Liz, smiled, and replied, "Yes, it was. I kept the dress all these years, hoping my daughter would wear it on her wedding day."

"Well, did Rachel, your daughter, wear your dress at her wedding?"

"She was seriously considering it. We had so much fun getting the dress out of the cedar-lined trunk and seeing her try it on. We were both surprised at how well it fit her. No alterations were needed; however, she needed lower-heeled shoes because she is two inches taller than me. Rachel appeared radiant in the dress; however, she selected to get a different dress. I understood as I wanted her to begin her marriage on a positive note and not wear a dress scared with painful memories."

It was Sydney's turn to want a snack and some water. "Grandma, may I have a snack and drink," asked Sydney.

"Sure thing," Martha replied as she began digging through the bag to find the bottled water and some crackers. Martha wiped Sydney's hands with a sanitizing wipe, told her to sit on the corner of the bench, and gave her a snack. Sydney was eating away and smiling like she had no care in the world. Martha enjoyed seeing this child's innocence and hoped she would remain this innocent as long as possible. "Are you done, Sydney?" asked Martha.

"Sure am, Grandma. Can I go back to the jungle gym?"

"Sure, have fun and be careful," Martha replied, as Sydney ran back to her friends.

A few minutes went by, and Liz broke the silence by asking Martha to tell her about her wedding day. "Did you have your nails and hair done? Tell me about your bachelorette party? Did you have fun?" asks Liz enthusiastically.

"To be honest," Martha said, "bachelorette parties were not the fad then. I had two showers thrown for me by family and friends. It was a bit awkward with my high school friends as they were studying, partying, and into the college scene. Here I was settling down. Do not get me wrong, the showers were nice, and I still have some of those gifts to this day. It quickly became evident that I was on a different road from my high school friends."

"What about your make-up and nails? How did you wear your hair?" asked Liz.

"Well, I kept that simple as I did my own hair and make-up. I had long hair back then and simply curled it. My nails were another matter," replied Martha. She continued, "Sam was adamant that I did not have any nail polish on my nails. Period. He became a little heated when I mentioned it, but I did get him to allow me to use clear nail polish. I have never liked my hands or nails; like any bride, I wanted to look and feel pretty. Sam relented to the clear nail polish when I pleaded my case."

Liz remarked, "Martha did you hear what you said?"

"What do you mean?"

"Martha, you just said that Sam 'allowed' you to wear the clear nail polish. I am bothered, Martha, by your choice of using the word 'allow.'"

"I see what you mean," Martha said. "All I can say is that is how I perceived it then and how I still feel about that incident. I had to get his permission to be pretty." Both women sat silently for the next few minutes replaying this in their minds.

Martha broke the silence. "One thing happened as I began walking down the aisle."

"What was that?" Liz asked.

"As my dad and I entered the church, my stomach flipped, and I grabbed tighter onto my dad's arm. He sensed it, glanced at me, and said, 'It is not too late to back out of this.' I was surprised at his statement, but as I turned and peered at the two hundred faces staring at me and knowing my parents had already spent money on this event, I told him I was doing this. I attributed my feelings to wedding day jitters."

Liz's mouth dropped, and she quickly regained her composure. "Wow," Liz said and continued. "I had the same thing happen to me as I started to walk down the aisle. What does this mean? Should I have married my husband?"

Martha looked at her, "Liz, that is not a question for me to answer. All I can do is tell my story. I have reflected on how my life would be if I had not married Sam, but it always comes back to the same thing. I would not have had these three children and grandchildren if it were not for Sam. I do not regret that part at all. But I believe that if we stray from the road God wants us to travel, He finds ways to get us back to Him. Just like the Bible story of the Good Shepherd looking for the one lost sheep. God found me and brought me back closer to Him. He has different plans for me."

The two women sat silent again and observed the kids play. They were having such a fun time. "Martha," Liz said, "How about the honeymoon! Did he plan a romantic get-away?"

Martha laughed, "Well, let's just say it wasn't what I expected."

"Oh no, what happened?"

Martha began, "Our wedding took place at 5 pm on a Friday and immediately following the service, there was the reception with a nice sit-down dinner at a beautiful country club that also included dancing to a live band. Sam made plans for the two of us to fly to San Francisco for the weekend. Between work and school schedules, this was what we could conceivably fit in our budget.

"We left after the reception, and I recall we got to the hotel in San Francisco around midnight. It was a bit late, but I wanted to take the entire day in and record the events in my mind. You only get married once! Well, I excused myself to take a quick shower, and ten minutes later,

I came out of the bathroom only to find Sam sound asleep. I tried to wake him but to no avail. So, I crawled into bed and went to sleep. That was not what I envisioned the wedding night to be. I was disappointed.

"The rest of the weekend went fine. We took in all the tourist sites like the Golden Gate Bridge, Fishermen's Wharf, a cable car ride, and went to Chinatown. We returned on Sunday afternoon to go back to work the next day."

Martha glanced at her watch and told Liz she had to get back home to begin dinner preparations and finish some chores. They called the kids to come back from the jungle gym. Everyone said their goodbyes and left for their respective homes.

Later that night, as everyone discussed their day at dinner, Sydney suddenly announced, "Grandma, you were laughing a couple of times today when I was playing on the jungle gym. What was so funny?"

Sydney's comment caught Rachel's attention, and she stared at Martha for her reaction. Rachel was protective of Martha and was looking for signs that her new friendship with Liz was not hurting her. Instead, Martha just smiled and told everyone they were sharing stories of raising kids including some funny antics kids are known to do. Then, everyone went back to eating dinner.

After dinner, Rachel sat next to her mom on the couch as she was crocheting her afghan. She asked her if her friendship with Liz was getting to be too much?

"This pain is in the past, and the pain has long since disappeared," Martha tells Rachel. "Time heals all wounds, so they say."

Rachel smiled and kissed her mom good night. Soon Martha retired to her room to do a little reading before turning out the light.

CHAPTER 7

EARTHQUAKE

Martha and Sydney spent the next few days home as the temperature was cooler and the wind was blowing. Unfortunately, they both suffered from allergies, and the wind worsened their condition. So instead, Martha had Sydney help her bake for an upcoming church function. The two made chocolate chip cookies, sugar cookies, snickerdoodles, brownies, and chocolate cupcakes. The sweet smell of these baked goods filled the house. Sydney had fun licking the bowl and putting the cookie dough on the baking sheet. Martha was always looking for ways to create memories with her grandkids – just like her mother did. No one can ever take away one's cherished memories.

Finally, the wind died down, and the temperature warmed up giving Martha and Sydney an opportunity to head for the park. Liz was not there, so Sydney went alone to the jungle gym as Martha sat on the bench to watch her play. About a half-hour later, Liz showed up with her kids, who took off to play. Liz sat down, and the two said hello and asked how the other was doing. Martha told Liz how she had been busy baking for an upcoming church function. Liz mentioned she had not been at the park as her husband came home from his trip, and things at home had been a little tense. The two women sat quietly on the bench, watching the kids play.

Unexpectedly, Liz asked Martha, "Did Sam ever hit you?"

After taking a deep breath, Martha replied, "Yes, once. Why do you ask?" Concerned that Liz's husband had hit her, she checked for bruises but did not see any.

Liz responded, "No, but he did get so angry that he put his fist through the wall. His temper frightens me. Do you mind telling me what happened with you and Sam?"

Martha began, "Sam and I had been married about a month. It was a Saturday afternoon. Sam had gone to work, and I was at home doing the Saturday chores. A small earthquake struck when Sam was working, and I got scared. I'm not too fond of earthquakes, and this one had a lot of rolling. I called my parents, who lived about 15 minutes away, to see if they had experienced it and were okay. About that time, Sam came home and asked who was on the phone. I told him, my parents, as there was just an earthquake. I observed him tense up, and he motioned for me to hang up the phone. I got off the call as quickly as possible.

"Next, I remember that he started yelling at me and told me I was never to call my parents. 'What did you say?' I asked him. 'You heard me,' he replied. I told him I was scared and that is why I called. He told me that I was to only reach out to him and no one else. I reminded him that he was unavailable, and with that statement, he slapped me across the face with the back of his hand and then subsequently put his fist through the wall. I was stunned. My dad never hit my mom or put his fist through the wall. I just stood there as fear immobilized me from moving or speaking.

"After realizing what he had done, Sam immediately apologized to me, asked my forgiveness, and promised it would not happen again."

"Did he keep his word?" asked Liz.

"Yes and no," replied Martha. "He didn't hit me again, but he beat one of my sons."

The two women sat in silence, absorbing what had transpired. Finally,

Martha said, "I also recall that my sister came to visit soon after the earthquake. She saw the hole and asked what had happened. I told her we were moving something that hit the wall and caused the hole. I lied because I was embarrassed and too proud to admit that I had made a mistake with this marriage. My sister just stared at me. I do not think she believed me, but she did not want to press this further. This incident caused me to wonder what I had done that was so wrong to get slapped. It was another attempt by Sam to cut me down as I struggled to learn the triggers to avoid upsetting him."

Again, silence ensued between the two women, and they both found some pleasure watching the children play. 'Their lives are so simple, so carefree. To be that young and happy again,' Martha thought.

Martha turned to Liz and asked her what made her husband upset.

"That is a good question. I am still trying to figure it out."

Martha asked her to go back and recount the incident with her.

Liz began, "He came home from work, and everything appeared to be fine as he told us hello and picked up each of the kids and kissed them. He went to the bedroom to change his clothes while I finished getting dinner on the table. We all sat down to eat. One of the kids whined about not liking their vegetables, and he went off. Yelling things like no one appreciates him, how he works hard and expects to have a quiet meal. He got up from the table and walked towards his home office, hitting the wall with his fist, resulting in the hole." Liz was visibly upset recounting this incident.

Martha asked how the kids reacted.

"They were dumbfounded, as was I."

"Something is going on with him," remarked Martha. "Liz, you did not do anything wrong. Please know this and, for God's sake, believe this. Your mental well-being is at stake."

Liz shook her head, agreeing with Martha's comment.

"Do you want to pray, Liz?"

"Yes."

The two women prayed for Liz's marriage, family, and health. Just then, all three kids came to the bench. They were hungry and wanted to go home to eat. Everyone said their goodbyes, and Martha told Liz to keep the faith, and Liz smiled.

Later that night, at dinner, when it came time for Sydney to talk about her day, she told everyone that Amy, Liz's daughter, told her that Amy's dad had gotten mad the night before and put a hole in the wall because she did not eat her vegetables. Martha's eyes opened wide, and she stared at Rachel, who had straightened up in her chair and glared at Martha.

"Hmm," said Rachel, "it seems like there may have been something else going on to get her dad upset. Please know that while your dad and I want you all to be healthy and strong, we would never get so mad as to put a hole in the wall."

Sydney glanced up at Rachel with her big brown eyes and said, "I know, Momma." Rachel stared at Martha with a look that said, 'We will talk about this later.'

With the kids upstairs ready for bed, Rachel approached Martha, sitting on the couch crocheting. "Mom," Rachel says, "I hope that the kids, particularly Sydney, are not overhearing the conversations you are having with Liz."

"Of course not! We stop talking before the kids are near us."

"Ok, I hoped so. But I wanted to be sure. Sounds like a sad situation."

"Yes, it is, and they need prayers."

"Sounds like that is all we can do."

Martha put her crocheting down, kissed Rachel good-night, and headed upstairs for the night. It took her a while to fall asleep while recounting the day's events. She feared she would soon have to tell Liz about her son, and she was not looking forward to it.

CHAPTER 8

CAR ACCIDENT

Martha and Sydney returned to the park the next day. Upon seeing Jess and Amy, Liz's kids, Sydney hugged them. Martha reminded Sydney that their time at the park would be less than the previous days as the cooler weather caused Martha's arthritis to flare up.

Sydney replied, "Ok, Grandma. I hope your knees get better while we are here." Martha thanked Sydney for her kindness.

Ever so curious, Liz asked Martha what was wrong with her knees. Martha explained that she was in a bad car accident in her early twenties, where she went through the windshield, shattering both of her kneecaps. Liz was shocked and asked Martha if there was a story to this. Martha smiles and asks Liz if she wants to hear it. Liz, of course, nods yes.

Martha begins, "Let's see. I had just turned twenty-two. Sam and I had been married about two and a half years. One fall day, Sam asked me to go to the desert while he did his job. I was reluctant to go because I had taken a week off work to catch up on some projects. He was insistent and told me that I was being selfish if I did not go, so I went. Since I was the passenger in the car, I brought along some small needlework projects to keep myself busy as Sam did his work. I recall visiting a couple of the larger country clubs in the desert and watched as Sam either installed tennis nets or measured for windscreens that would go along the fence perimeter of the tennis courts. He completed his work, and we left the area mid-afternoon. Sam decided to take a different route home and we found ourselves on a two-lane highway in the desert. There was a vehicle in front of us that we had been following at a safe distance for several miles. Upon coming to a crossroad, the vehicle signaled with their car blinker that they were turning right. Sam slowed down to keep the safe distance. What we did not expect was that the vehicle turned right but then made an immediate U-turn on that road which positioned him coming back on the road we were on. Rather than stopping to re-enter the highway we were traveling on, the vehicle kept going and hit us on the right front passenger side of our vehicle. I went through the windshield, but Sam stayed inside the vehicle as it rolled a couple of times to a stop."

Liz's jaw dropped, "Oh my, this is horrible. What happened next?"

Martha continued, "I remember waking up on the road. Sam was holding my chin as he worried my jugular vein was severed and did not want me to bleed out. I observed a cut on his forehead and told him he was hurt, but he replied he was fine.

"The paramedics arrived and took over, first asking me questions like my name, date, time of day, and if I knew what happened. They were checking for a head injury, but fortunately, I answered everything correctly. Those moments were very surreal as I did not feel any pain. I had no idea the trauma my legs endured until they went to lift me on the gurney. Talk about excruciating pain! It was horrible. I remember screaming when they moved me. The paramedics transported me to the local hospital. Although I do not remember much, the doctor determined I needed more medical treatment than they could conceivably provide and arranged transportation to a larger hospital nearby."

"What happened next?" asked Liz.

"The ambulance finally came to transport me to the larger hospital. Since our vehicle was totaled, Sam had no transportation and the ambulance driver allowed him to travel inside the ambulance.

I remember it being dark when we arrived., Sam's boss came to take him home just as we arrived. Sam was lucky. He sustained some small cuts and bruises and walked away from the accident. I, on the other hand, was not so lucky!" Sam decided to go home with his boss, leaving me alone at the hospital, which was a few hours away from our home. I remember being in pain and feeling abandoned. I was disappointed that Sam didn't stay to provide me with some support."

"Wait," Liz interrupted, "he left you alone in the hospital?"

"He sure did," replied Martha as her voice reflected the disappointment she faced with Sam's action. "That was a long night. Doctors and nurses kept coming in and out of the ER room. Because I had indicated that I wanted to be seen by my doctor, they were unsure whether to admit me to their hospital. So, I waited all night to finally learn they decided to admit me. The ambulance transport needed to get back to where I lived, about two and a half hours away from the desert and would not be available until Sunday. The car accident happened on a Thursday afternoon. Hearing that I would be spending Friday and Saturday in the hospital, without any medical treatment on my knees which had been shattered, was a bitter disappointment. It also meant that I would be in that hospital, all alone and in pain, for a few more days. I was devastated."

"That's a long time," Liz responded. Martha shook her head in agreement.

"As I said, doctors and nurses were in and out until I got to my room. At one point, a plastic surgeon stitched up my chin and forehead, which sustained deep cuts. He told me he would not give me anything to numb the area, as is typically done when getting stitches. I remember asking him why. He indicated that the head injury prevented him from doing so as it would have negative consequences. When I pressed him about a head injury, the doctor indicated that anytime someone hits their head, they are observed for a minimum of 24 hours. While I knew the answers to the questions the paramedics asked and was fully aware of my surroundings, the doctor said he was erring on the side of caution because of the cuts on my head.

"He then told me to brace myself as it would hurt. I remember thinking, 'More pain? Great – just what I needed.' Fortunately, a male nurse was kind and told me to squeeze his hand during this process. Oh, and I did. I only hope that I did not break the bones in his hand. I still remember the needle going in and out for each stitch. In and out, then in and out. Each time feeling the prick of the needle as it entered and exited the wound. And so, it continued, and I ended up with about thirty stitches." Martha's eyes welled up with tears.

Liz told her to take a break and drink some water. Martha gets some bottled water from her bag and takes some sips.

After calming down, Martha continued, "At one point, I stared at my hands and arms, which sustained cuts and scrapes and covered with road debris. I touched my hair, only to feel the dried-up blood. My hair was a very tangled, messy rat's nest. Not only was I in pain, but disgustingly dirty and I reflected on what I did to deserve this. Finally, after I was wheeled into my room, a nurse took the time to painstakingly wash my hair and cleaned me up as best as she could."

"How long did it take to recover from these injuries?" asked Liz.

"A long time," replied Martha. "The day I was transported back to the hospital near my home, the ambulance I was in had a flat tire. I could sense that the ambulance driver was going faster than the posted speed limit as the gurney had me facing towards the back window. The ambulance was in the fast lane and passing other vehicles. Suddenly the ambulance began to swerve erratically, and I thought I was going to be in another accident. The driver got the ambulance under control and pulled off to the emergency lane located along the fast lane of the freeway. The driver then announced that one of the tires blew out.

"October is still a hot month in the desert, so we were all on the side of the road waiting for the tire to get fixed. They kept me inside the ambulance, on the gurney, and doing their best to keep the vehicle cool inside. Unfortunately, the ambulance did not have a spare tire. The area in the vehicle where it should have been, did not contain one, so the driver had to call his office to get a spare tire. I don't know why another ambulance wasn't immediately called to transfer me, and I never got a clear answer to this question.

"Eventually, a company representative showed up with a spare tire and the ambulance driver began to change the tire. A decision was made to keep me inside while the tire was being changed. However, as the tire was being removed, the hub cap rolled across the four-lane highway. Rather than just leaving it, the ambulance driver decided to cross all four lanes to retrieve it, dodging cars along the way. I felt like I was in an old slapstick comedy movie as the comedy of errors on the part of the ambulance driver just kept coming. I did my best to remain as calm as I could. I knew getting upset wasn't going to help me or the situation, and all I wanted was to just go home. Sam was driving my vehicle and was behind the ambulance when this happened, so he observed it all."

Martha stopped speaking to take some sips of water.

"Oh, and I forgot to add that Sam did not tell my parents of the accident until the day after it happened. My folks were livid with him, and they immediately came out to visit me in the desert."

Liz looked at Martha in shock and told her that she could not believe what Martha went through.

"Yes, it was quite the adventure," Martha quips. "I did need knee surgery on both legs as they had to remove the shattered kneecaps, but the doctor decided to wait until the exterior wounds began healing to avoid getting an infection in my bones. It was about three weeks after the accident before they performed this surgery. The surgery took almost three hours, and the doctor told my parents I would be in much pain after the surgery. One of my mom's closest friends began to pray with my mom that I would be spared any pain and prayed for complete and quick healing. I had no pain that night and did not require pain medication afterward. I acknowledged that God was with me and had not abandoned me."

Martha paused and drank some water. Recalling this memory moved Martha to tears as she appreciated how much God has been with her throughout her life.

"However," Martha continued, "I had an allergic reaction to an antibiotic given to me during the surgery that was needed to prevent infection. I was in the hospital for several more weeks after the surgery. The doctor wanted to keep me in longer, but it was getting close to Thanksgiving. I emphatically told the doctor that I was not having turkey dinner in the hospital and asked what I had to do to get out. I was done with the hospital and wanted to go home.

"It took two more knee surgeries, a plastic surgery, and a year and a half of physical therapy before I regained my mobility. I had to learn how to walk again. And while I was not clear to drive, Sam refused to take me to physical therapy after a few weeks as it was too much of an inconvenience for him to do so. As soon as I had enough mobility in my knees to where I felt I could safely drive, I began driving myself to my appointments and arranged times to attend therapy when less cars were on the road. Not an ideal situation but I was determined to get my life back, even if I had to do it all by myself. All I can say is that it is easier for small kids to learn to walk than it is as an adult."

Liz laughed at this last comment as she appreciated Martha's sense of humor.

Martha glanced at her watch and stated, "Oh my gosh, look at the time! I need to start heading home." Liz acknowledged the time and said she planned on staying another twenty minutes. Martha then said, "Liz, I am so sorry. I have been so caught up in today's discussion that I forgot to ask you how things are at home."

Liz replied, "It is better. I spoke to my husband, and he admitted there are some pressures from the work he is handling. And he expressed sorrow about yelling at the kids and did apologize to them last night at dinner."

"Well, that's a start!" replied Martha. "Keep praying for him! Why don't you and your family join us at our weekend church festival? There are rides, games, and lots of family fun."

Liz said that she would think about it. Martha provided her with the church's phone number to get more information. With that, they said farewell, and Martha and Sydney headed home.

That night at dinner, Rachel asked Martha how Liz was doing. Martha said she appeared happier today, but she would keep praying for them. Then, the conversation turned to the upcoming church festival and what everyone would do to prepare for it. Again, the discussion was lively as everyone was excited to attend the event.

After dinner, Martha said goodnight to everyone. Her arthritis was still bothering her, and she mostly wanted some alone time to process recalling the car accident. It was a tough time in her life, but Martha concluded early on that God was not done with her yet. So, she meditated on what else God had in store for her. And, with that thought, she wandered off to sleep.

CHAPTER 9

FIRST BORN

Martha and Rachel spent the next couple of days putting the finishing touches on the kids' costumes. Sarah, Michael, and Sydney were excited and kept asking when they could try on their costumes. One or all of them were asking this question every five minutes. "Not yet" is the answer Rachel and Martha were constantly telling them. Soon enough, the festival day arrived, and everyone got dressed in anticipation of a fun and exciting day. Finally, the family piled into the car and headed to the church.

Parking proved to be a bit challenging, as it usually was, for church events. It's nice seeing so many families come together and spend time with one another. Soon James found a parking spot at the very end of the lot, and everyone made their way to the games. They all participated in playing some games, but it was Michael who earned the most prizes for winning. Rachel asked James to take the kids to the area to get their costumes judged because she wanted to take Martha to the craft section to see what items were on display. Rachel and Martha studied the various crocheted and knitted items. There were some needlepoint and cross stitch items as well.

Rachel glanced at Martha and said, "Mom, I don't know why you don't enter this. Your work is every bit as beautiful as these items."

"Thanks, Rachel, but I prefer making useful things or giving them away as gifts. I don't need a prize." Rachel hugged her, and they left to join

James and the kids.

Michael was the first to spot Rachel and Martha. Running up to them, he proudly yelled, "Mom, Mom, look what I won." Michael was grinning from ear to ear while holding up the blue second-place ribbon.

"That's fantastic," Rachel said. She took the ribbon and held it up for a closer view. She showed it to Martha. Both women smiled at each other and then smiled back at Michael, dressed as Blackbeard, the pirate. His costume was easy enough to make, but Rachel did a fantastic job on his make-up which surely cinched the win.

Rachel asked Sarah and Sydney how they did. Each of them showed off their yellow ribbon for participating. Sarah was dressed as Pocahontas, while Sydney came as Belle from *Beauty and the Beast*. Neither were bothered that they didn't win, which was a good thing.

Suddenly Sydney calls out, "Grandma, look! There's Amy and Jess!" Martha turns around and saw Liz with her family. It was good to see that Liz's husband came with them.

Seeing Martha, Liz walked up to her and introduced her husband, Jeff. Next, Martha introduced Liz to James and Rachel. After the introductions, they all agreed to stand in line for some food.

Martha observed that Jeff was tall and slender. He had dark, straight hair with piercing blue eyes that showed off his perfectly white, straight teeth when he smiled. Jeff was handsome, and Martha understood Liz's attraction for him. They looked like a couple who belonged together.

Rachel points to a little boy running by and says, "Mom, do you remember when Nick wore that same Ninja Turtle costume?"

Martha laughed and replied, "Sure do!" Liz wondered who Nick was as Martha had not mentioned him. She planned on asking Martha about Nick when the time was more appropriate. Seeing James with the kids, Rachel announced that she needed to use the restroom and inquired if Martha or Liz wanted to join her. They both agreed to join her but only after Liz checked to see that Jeff was with her kids. Upon making their way back from the restroom, Rachel noticed an empty pavilion and seeing that the husbands were still with the kids, Rachel asked Martha if she wanted to sit for a couple of minutes. Martha agreed. Liz saw this as an opportunity to ask about Nick so she asked if she could join them. Martha and Rachel wholeheartedly agreed.

Not able to contain her curiosity any longer, Liz asked "Who's Nick?"

Martha replied, "Nick is Rachel's older brother and my first born. I became pregnant with him between knee surgeries. It was difficult to determine a due date for his arrival because the accident impacted my menstrual cycle. The best guess was the first week or two in September – close to my birthday. However, he ended up coming sooner than planned, and where we believed he was two and a half weeks early, the pediatrician said he was premature and estimated to be six weeks early. That was shocking. He came in at six pounds, six ounces, and twenty and three-quarters inches long. Quite honestly, I was happy that he wasn't bigger because this was the first-time giving birth, and I had no idea what to expect. I was so thankful that he was born naturally and not through Caesarian section."

Liz stared at Martha and asked, "Naturally? Didn't you have an epidural or anything?"

Martha replied, "No, it was all-natural. That was the 'thing' to do then. The choice was between the Lamaze or Bradley method of breathing. Sam selected the Bradley method. When I questioned him about it, he said I had no choice. I was a bit miffed as I hadn't even had time to research it. At any rate, the irony was that I have used the Bradley method many times since, especially with dental work!"

Rachel and Liz laughed as Martha continued, "I was lucky that the labor was not long. When I got to the hospital, they determined I was ready to deliver and rushed me to the delivery room. Because my knees would not bend to use the stir-ups effectively, they had me deliver on my side. It didn't matter to me as long as there was no negative impact on the baby. Soon, he was born, and the nurses placed him in my arms. Sam was in the room with me. He began to cry at seeing his son, who resembled him with his dark hair and eyes. When I held Nick, this incredible emotional bonding occurred. I was overwhelmed with the pure joy and love I had for him. What a miracle!"

Rachel and Liz smiled as Martha talked about Nick. The three began to share their childbirth stories as only women can, but all agreed that giving birth was a true gift from God that only women are lucky enough to participate!

The kids finished their dinner and begged their parents to play more games before the night ended. Finally, the two families went their separate ways, and it was time for James and Rachel to take everyone home. Sarah, Michael, and Sydney were busy chatting in the car on the way home, comparing all their winnings and trying to find ways to swap one winning prize for another. Martha just smiled and enjoyed the interaction. She was glad that Liz and her family came and hoped this might be what was needed to get their marriage back on track.

CHAPTER 10

ON THE MOVE

The following day, Martha was the first to wake up. She went downstairs, made herself a cup of tea, and went outside and sat in her favorite chair on the front porch. The sun was beginning to rise, and the birds chirped away with a tune only they would recognize. Martha sipped her tea and took in the sounds of a new morning.

—

Her mind wandered to the night before and how much fun the kids had. 'It's so important to create these memories for the kids,' Martha believed. She was glad Liz came with her family and hoped they enjoyed themselves. She recalled the little boy in the Ninja Turtle costume, thinking about Nick. He was fifty-two and living back east. Nick has had the most challenging time moving past the divorce of her three kids. He chose to live with his dad at the time of the divorce as the state determined he was of age to make that decision. Nick will never admit to making the wrong choice, but this was his choice. Martha understood why Nick made it as he was always Sam's favorite, and Sam had a way of giving in to what Nick wanted, even at the expense of his siblings. As far as Nick was concerned, he knew how to manipulate his father. Nick believed his life would be better staying with his dad, which proved not to be the case.

Not long after Nick was born, Sam had completed college. While the plan was for Martha to finish her degree when Sam had completed his studies, the goal never came to fruition. Once Nick was born, the family moved to the south. That was where Sam's family moved a year before Nick's birth after they agreed they no longer liked living in California. Sam desperately missed his family, and Martha reluctantly made the move. Fortunately, Sam quickly got a job managing a branch with a national car rental company. The hours were brutal – six days a week, twelve hours a day. Martha hardly ever interacted with Sam, and she concentrated on raising Nick.

After about a year and a half, Sam wanted to change jobs and found a marketing job with a national computer firm. It was a sales position which meant more traveling. The firm relocated the family to a town in Texas. Sam quickly bonded with his fellow sales associates while Martha felt more alone than ever. Nick was getting to the age where he would attend pre-school during the day, so Martha began looking for work. She landed a job interview, but when it was time to leave to meet the potential new employer, Sam told her that it was not a good idea and that her job was to take care of Nick, keep the house clean, and keep his shirts clean and pressed. Martha was devastated. Her only interaction with adults occurred when Sam invited these two single salesmen over for dinner periodically for a home-cooked meal. Seeing these two guys enjoy a home-cooked meal made her smile. At least her cooking was not that bad because they gobbled it like there was no tomorrow. On the other hand, Sam complained about her cooking every chance he got. Even when she prepared a dish he requested, he still found an excuse to complain and make her feel that this was another thing she could not do.

Martha longed for some adult interaction. She found ways to keep herself busy by reading novels and teaching herself new craft skills. When Nick was not in pre-school, she spent quite a bit of time reading to him, teaching him the alphabet, and learning to count. Nick was smart and picked up these skills quickly. But keeping busy didn't fill her need for adult interaction. What made matters worse was that she could not rely on a church community. Several months after they married, Sam believed there was no need to attend church. He believed that one did not need to attend church to believe in God. Martha continued to attend church for a while, but after the car accident, going to church was impossible as Sam would not drive her there. Discouraged, she eventually gave up going to church.

Ironically, after Nick was born, Sam was insistent that Nick get baptized Lutheran, even though Sam agreed to have all children from this marriage baptized Catholic. Martha thought this might be an opportunity to become involved with church, even if it was not the Catholic church. The most important thing for Martha, however, was that Nick be baptized, at least, he would be a Christian. Unfortunately, her hope was quickly dashed for becoming involved with a church community as Sam's focus was the baptism and nothing further. Even though Martha was faithful in prayer for many years, she floundered with having an authentic relationship with God. As a result, she missed going to church to get the connection she was truly craving from other believers and from God.

After a few years in Texas, Sam earned a promotion and a trip with other top salespeople to a lake resort. Spouses were encouraged to go, but it left Sam and Martha with the dilemma of finding a sitter for Nick for a few days. Unfortunately, Sam's parents were not able to help, so it was Martha's sister who flew to Texas from Los Angeles for sitter duty. Martha was happy to see her sister, Mary, as it had been a couple of years. Although Sam, Martha, and Nick drove once a month to see Sam's family, Martha was not allowed to fly to California to see her family. Sam told her they were not able to afford it. Sam was faithful to his family and called weekly, usually on weekends, but Martha was allowed one call per month to her family, and her mom would do the calling to check-in.

The lake trip was less than spectacular. Martha had recently purchased some white flip-flops for the beach at the lake. Sam took one look at them and threw them out the window. He cut the trip short using an issue with Nick as an excuse to leave early. It was a long drive home for Martha as all Sam did was complain about how she appeared, dressed, and acted. She sat there in silence; stunned and confused. She just didn't understand what she did or said that was so awful or wrong to make Sam react in this manner. When they returned home, Mary was surprised to see them both and asked if everything was okay. Sam told some fabricated lie to Mary, but she was watching Martha's reaction. She watched her sister's eyes shifting downward but let it go and soon flew back to Los Angeles.

That Christmas, Martha's family came to Texas to visit. Everyone, including Sam, had a wonderful time. When it was time for them to leave, Martha was sad and admitted to Sam how miserable she was with no support system. He appeared sympathetic. To her surprise, a couple of months later, Martha's father offered Sam a partnership in the family business. Sam jumped at this opportunity, and the family moved back to California. Martha was thrilled!

—

Martha was startled awake by the thud of a door closing. She realized she had dozed off with her memories of the past. Looking at her watch, she noticed it was time to get ready for church. She had lector duty and needed to be at church a few minutes early. The morning chaos of eating breakfast and getting dressed ensued, and soon all of them piled into the car, and they drove off to attend church.

CHAPTER 11

FAMILY BUSINESS

The church, packed with attendees, left a few empty seats for the late comers to Mass. Martha was grateful that her selected reading as lector went off without a hitch. Despite her fear of public speaking and discomfort with being the center of attention, she found lector's duty inspiring. She forgot that she was standing before hundreds of people with all eyes on her as she read a scriptural passage. She was inspired to work in this ministry and has enjoyed doing so for many years.

After Mass, the family went for their traditional lunch at one of the kid's favorite restaurants. Each week, James had the kids take turns picking the restaurant. Today, it was Michael's turn to choose, which he did, and James headed the car in that direction. Martha enjoyed these weekly lunches. She loved the interaction James and Rachel had with their kids. They talked about the upcoming week and made mental notes of exams the kids would take, forthcoming sporting events where transportation was needed, and attendance warranted. Finally, after synchronizing the activities into the family calendar, James took everyone home.

—

James and the kids spent the afternoon playing kickball while Martha surveilled the activity from her favorite front porch chair. While watching them, her mind wandered off, and she reflected on those years with Sam helping her parents in the family business. Those were good years, and everyone was happy. Life was good.

One day, Paul had a massive heart attack at age fifty-two. While it was touch and go for a few days, he survived, but the doctors could not get to the damaged areas to clear the blockage. Paul lived with this issue for the rest of his life. His heart was only operating at about forty percent of its capacity. Despite this challenge, Paul worked to overcome this health challenge and made the most of each day.

Not long after this occurred, Martha learned she was pregnant with her second child. The pregnancy was excellent news as Sam and Martha had been trying for several years to conceive again. However, around the fourth month of the pregnancy, Martha began bleeding, and there was concern that she would miscarry. Fortunately, that did not happen, and she carried her second son, Jeremy, to term. Labor and delivery were normal, and Jeremy came in at eight pounds, twelve ounces, and twenty-one inches long. As soon as Sam saw him, his comment was, "He certainly doesn't look like Nick!" He turned and walked out of the room. The nurse put Jeremy into her arms and immediately observed his red hair and blue eyes. Jeremy's appearance made her smile. While Martha's hair eventually turned from red, at her birth, to dishwater blonde, Jeremy's hair did the same, but, like Martha, he kept his bright blue eyes.

As Jeremy grew, Martha noticed that Sam pulled away from any interaction with Jeremy and concentrated his free time with Nick. Sam got Nick involved with the Boy Scouts and all that entailed – notably, the Pinewood Derby and popcorn sales. At first, Martha was happy that Sam was getting involved with Nick but began to get concerned when Sam spent a lot of time with one of the Den Mothers and her family. When Martha brought it up, Sam told her that the friendship was "no big deal" and not to be concerned. In the meantime, Sam avoided interacting with Jeremy, who enjoyed spending his time outdoors. If Jeremy could live outside, he would have. He had two favorite pastimes – mowing the backyard with his plastic toy lawn mower and watching the trash trucks pick up the neighborhood trash every Tuesday. Jeremy would walk the cul-de-sac, following the trash truck while it picked up everyone's trash. The neighbors got a big chuckle out of this. Martha never figured out the fascination with the trash truck, but Jeremy was mesmerized by the process.

Martha noticed as time passed that Sam became more distant and frustrated with the simplest things. He began to take his frustrations out on the family dog, Smokey, who was about eight years old. Martha received Smokey as a gift soon after they were married, and she loved that dog. Smokey was there by her side as she recuperated from the car accident, and he became very protective of her. He was a little thing, weighing about ten pounds, but he was full of life and personality. But her heart broke every time Sam would pull his ears, making him yelp in a horrible high-pitched sound. It was getting to the point where Smokey was snapping back at Sam, causing more angst for everyone, including Smokey.

One day, Ray, a former colleague of Sam's, came to visit. He spent a couple of days in the guest bedroom, and it was during this time that Martha was busy putting the finishing touches on Nick's upcoming birthday party. The night before Nick's party, Sam began pulling Smokey's ears, Smokey snapped back, and Sam kicked him across the room. It was awful. The next day, as Ray talked to Martha's parents, he was asked how he was enjoying California. Ray replied that he liked the visit but said, "Smokey didn't have a good night last night." There was dead silence.

The birthday party went on as scheduled, but Martha was upset with how Sam was treating Smokey and recognized it was not only wrong but not a good example to set for Nick and Jeremy. A few days later, Martha made the decision to put Smokey down. She loved him too much to let him suffer and wouldn't give him away for fear that his trauma would be too much for another family who would either not want to adopt him or put him down. She took Smokey to the vet while Sam was at work. That evening, Sam asked where the dog was. Martha told him what she had done. Sam was stunned and then asked why. With tears streaming from her eyes, she told him that she couldn't stand him being hurt anymore and didn't want him to suffer continually. They didn't speak to each other the rest of the night.

Years later, Martha's mom reminded her of the words she used when she told her what had happened. Those words were, "I think I got rid of the wrong one."

A couple of months later, Sam mentioned possibly getting another dog. Martha said she didn't want another pet and that two kids were enough to look after. He disagreed and reminded Martha of being a dog lover. While that was true, she reminded him that she wasn't interested. The next day Sam brought home not only one puppy but two of them. He was trying to make up with Martha, but he didn't understand that this wasn't going to cut it. So, they kept the dogs, and Martha, of course, loved them. But when it came time to leave the marriage, she left the dogs with Sam.

Being a dog lover, the decision to leave the dogs behind was not an easy one but she had two important reasons for doing so. The first reason was it was her way to get back at Sam for getting the dogs in the first place after she had stated she didn't want to replace Smokey. The second reason was that the new apartment required a large pet deposit and, quite simply, she didn't have the funds for the deposit.

—

The aroma of the hamburgers barbequing on the grill brought Martha back from her thoughts. She quickly got up and went to the kitchen to help Rachel finish preparations. Soon it was time to sit down and eat.

James prayed a blessing over the food before they enjoyed their burgers. After dinner, the family sat down to play a few games of 'Go Fish.' The evening quickly passed, and it was time for Martha to return to her room and head to bed. A new school week would begin tomorrow, and it promised to be busy.

CHAPTER 12

FIRE

A few days passed before Martha and Sydney found their way back to the park. Liz was sitting on the beige wooden bench when they arrived, talking on the phone. Next to her was a pen and pad of paper. Sydney went off to play with Jess and Amy. Martha sat on the bench next to Liz, and both women exchange smiles. Martha didn't want to interrupt Liz's conversation.

Soon Liz hung up and blurted out, "What a mess! We had a kitchen fire, and I can't believe all the calls to the insurance company, the contractors, etc. that I have had to make."

Shocked, Martha replied, "What? A fire? Is everyone okay? Oh my, this is horrible!"

Turning to face Martha on the bench, Liz described what had happened. Liz had been making tacos, and the stove's grease unexpectedly caught fire. She tried to douse the flames, but when it didn't work, she called 911, grabbed the kids, and got out of the house. While it felt like an eternity before the fire department arrived, it was only a couple of minutes. As she waited for help, she called her husband, who immediately came home.

"I am so sorry this has happened," Martha told her empathetically.

"Thanks, Martha. We were lucky that the fire only impacted the kitchen. The rest of the house is fine, but the inside wreaks of smoke."

"How can I help?" asked Martha.

"Well, I don't know. We have everything under control. The restoration company is removing the smoke smell from the house while the kids and I are at a hotel. Jeff is out of town this week. When the restoration company completes its work, we can live in the house while the kitchen is repaired."

"What about your meals? I am assuming you are eating out?"

Liz told her that the hotel room had a small kitchenette where she was making breakfast and lunch but that they were going out to eat for dinner.

"That makes sense. It sounds like you have it all under control! But I will talk to James and Rachel about inviting you all to Sunday dinners until your kitchen returns to where you can cook again. Then, you all can come over, and the kids can play in the yard and have a fun time." Martha conveyed to Liz, smiling.

Liz told her she appreciated the offer.

It was getting closer to noon, and the sun was becoming more intense. All three kids came over to get some water and snacks and then went back to the jungle gym. Martha sensed the wooden park bench's hardness getting to her back, and she stood up to stretch. Memories of the fire in her house many years ago came flooding back. Liz asked her if everything was okay. Martha told her she had the same thing happen a year before Rachel was born.

"What? You had a fire in your home, too?" asked Liz.

Martha slowly shook her head yes and began to tell the story. "Sam had been staining some wood in the backyard and left the rag outside to air dry. That night, he checked on the rag, and seeing that it was dry and no longer wreaked of the stain smell, he put the rag inside a five-gallon bucket in the garage. It was the only item inside the bucket. Around 2:00 am, I woke up to the sound of Pop! Pop! Pop! Thinking the sound was gunshots, I quickly woke up Sam and told him to get up because someone was shooting outside.

"The sound of knock, knock, knock made me realize someone was outside our front door. A neighbor yelled at us that the house was on fire. Sam got Nick while I got Jeremy, and we ran downstairs to get outside. The neighbor had already called the fire department, and the sounds of the sirens indicated the fire trucks were nearby. Another neighbor was kind enough to move his vehicle across the street so that I had a place to sit with the kids and stay warm. They provided us with blankets and warm drinks. Sam stayed outside while I sat in the backseat with the kids, hugging them and praying. I was so thankful we were alive.

"Fortunately, it wasn't long before the fire was out, but, like you, we were not allowed to go back inside, so one of the neighbors invited us in. Sam and I slept on their sleeper couch while the boys slept on the floor below in a sleeping bag.

"The firefighters contained the fire to the garage. The laundry room led from the family room to the garage, where the contractor found a cheap white plastic cross on the top of the door jamb that said 'Jesus Saves' in blue letters. I forgot that I had put that there. A few months prior, I received one of those solicitations to donate money, and inside was this cross. Something told me not to throw it out, but I didn't know where to put it, so I stuck it in the door jamb in the laundry room that led to the garage. While that laundry room door had minor smoke damage, the fire did not go past that door. When the contractor handed me that cross, his words were, 'He certainly does.'"

Martha had tears in her eyes recounting this latter part as it reminded her how much God loves her. That little plastic white cross is still in her possession.

Liz was silent, absorbing the words that Martha conveyed. "Wow! That's quite an experience."

Martha took a deep breath and replied, "Yes, it was! It turned out to be a blessing in disguise."

"How is that?"

"Well, I became pregnant with Rachel immediately after that incident. Apparently, I need to have stressful situations occur to get pregnant." Both women stared at each other and began laughing hysterically. Liz liked how Martha made light of life's challenging situations and how she assumed to just go with the flow.

"I bet you and Sam were excited about a little girl?" Liz asked.

"We didn't know we would have a girl until she was born. It was a great surprise." Then, Martha stopped talking and focused on Sydney, who was still having fun playing with Jess and Amy.

"What's wrong, Martha? Why did you stop talking about Rachel's birth?"

"Looking back, it was the beginning of the end and a definite turning point in my life."

CHAPTER 13

SACRIFICIAL LAMB

"What do you mean the beginning of the end?" Liz exclaimed.

"You will have to bear with me for this, Liz. It is something that I still feel guilty about to this very day." Martha replied.

"Take your time with this, Martha. I have some time before I need to go home,"

"About a few months before Rachel was born, Sam and I got a note from Nick's school asking us to talk to him about a minor infraction. I don't even remember what it was all about, but I just remember that something happened that warranted a teacher's note. At any rate, I was getting Jeremy ready for bed in his bedroom when I overheard Nick screaming, 'Don't, Daddy!' Slam went the door as Sam took Nick into our bathroom and began beating him with a belt. Leaving Jeremy in his crib with the rail up, I ran to the bathroom as quickly as possible and opened the door to catch Sam whipping Nick with the belt. I was shocked to see Nick standing half-naked in the bathtub with welts forming on his back from the continued whipping. I screamed at Sam and begged him to stop. I then stared at Nick and saw those light brown eyes filled with tears looking at me as if to say, 'Mom, why did you allow this to happen?' Sam walked out of the bathroom, and I did my best to comfort Nick and treat the wounds." Martha paused. Tears were in her eyes as she recounted this horrific event.

Liz grabbed Martha's hand telling her to take her time.

After a few moments, Martha began speaking again. "I spent the rest of the evening comforting Nick and Jeremy and finally got them both to bed. I wanted nothing to do with Sam. I was scared – scared for me, for Nick, for Jeremy, and my unborn child. I felt helpless, alone, and confused. 'Why did this happen?' I kept asking myself. I perceived I couldn't say anything to anyone as it would trigger another anger outburst leading to worse results. I laid in bed replaying Nick's little face in my head, repeatedly, like it was a broken record. I betrayed him by not protecting him, and I would not forgive myself for letting it happen. Sam later confessed to me how sorry he was and that he wouldn't do it again. I had heard those words before. But he did repeat his actions. Not with me this time, but with our son."

"Martha, oh Martha," Liz cried. "You were in a tricky situation, and this wasn't your fault. It's horrible what Sam did, but you didn't beat Nick – Sam did!"

Martha shook her head in agreement. "I know," Martha continued. "Many years later, a priest told me that chains were binding me when I went to confession. He suggested that I petition the church for an annulment. I was surprised that this was an option because of the time I was married and the length of time since I legally divorced. The priest assured me that the Church took these cases and granted annulments. It took me a month to request the paperwork and several more months before submitting it to the parish priest."

Liz interrupted, "Martha, did you find those chains?"

"I sure did," Martha responded. "It was the night I wrote about this incident in the annulment petition. I acknowledged that the chains were that I needed to forgive myself. God had long forgiven me. I needed to do it for myself."

"And have you?"

Martha replied. "Nick and I have spoken about this incident since then, and we are on excellent terms. Now that he is older, he better understands this incident and has long since forgiven me."

"That's good to hear, Martha," Liz said and continued, "So why was Sam so angry? Why was he so unhappy? What was going on at that time?"

Martha shrugged her shoulders as if she didn't know but then responded, "That's a great question. I remember that Sam and my dad were not getting along then, negatively impacting the business. However, he was still very friendly with the Den Mother from the Boy Scouts. Years later, my parents told me that Sam would spend hours at the mall rather than go to the office and work. I know he was also missing his family, and when his mother came out for Rachel's birth, as she did for Nick's and Jeremy's birth, she somehow talked him into moving back east."

Liz stopped Martha to ask about her family's involvement in her children's birth. "They weren't involved," Martha stated.

Liz's jaw dropped, "What?"

"That's right," Martha said, "He only called them after the kids were born, and they would come to visit in the hospital, but he never notified them when I went into labor."

Liz shook her head in disbelief. "That's cold."

"I agree," said Martha. "About a month after Rachel was born, we sold the house and moved back east to be near his family."

Liz looked at her watch and said it was time to go. Martha indicated it was her time to leave as well. They called the kids to return, and all went back to their respective homes. Sydney was tired from the park and slept longer than usual for her afternoon nap. This extra time allowed Martha to catch up on the laundry and regroup. The discussion today was challenging, but she was glad she got through it. Time has healed most of the wounds, but she wondered if it would ever heal all of them.

CHAPTER 14

TRAVELING SALESMAN

Later that night, Martha went outside to sit on the front porch to finish watching the sunset. With dinner finished and dishes washed, Rachel was busy with the kids getting them ready for bed. The temperature was cooling outside but not to the point of needing a sweater. Martha marveled at the sky with its red, orange, and purple colors painted across the western sky. She observed a sense of peace. Her mind began to wander back to Liz's earlier discussion. It was still heavy on her heart, and she reflected more on that time in her life. Could she have done anything differently?

Martha wandered back to when they moved back east right after Rachel was born. Sam quickly found a job, and the family moved to a neighborhood that backed up to one of several Civil War battlefields. Their new home was 1800 square feet, single-story, with a two-car garage, converted to a tuck-under basement. Inside the house was a large great room, formal dining room, kitchen eating area, three bedrooms, and two bathrooms. Since the home's exterior was peach in color with white trim, the kids affectionately referred to it as the 'peach house.' Two large bay windows, as well as a large porch, graced the front of the home. It was a beautiful home, and Martha hoped they would all be happy here. Unfortunately, this happiness was short-lived.

One day, when Martha returned from shopping, she found her mother-in-law, Theresa, in the dining room wallpapering the walls. On her own accord, Theresa had purchased wallpaper without asking if the pattern would be something Sam and Martha would like. Martha was shocked. She sensed she was obligated to say she liked it but was appalled that Theresa took it upon herself to interfere with decorating her home. This interference would continue for the next few years and manifest itself by criticism should Theresa find a handprint on the wall or an item out of place. These actions would contribute to the erosion of Martha's self-esteem and belief that anything she would do was suitable. When Martha mentioned this interference to Sam, he responded that his mother was being helpful and that she should appreciate it. However, he did not understand that it eroded her confidence to be a good homemaker and make the home they would be proud of living in.

With Sam's busy work schedule, Martha found time to meet some neighbors and joined the board of directors of their homeowner's association (HOA). Little did she know, but her involvement with the HOA would lead her to a new career path in the future. Martha enjoyed spending time with her neighbor across the street, Kim Johnson. Kim was shorter than Martha and had jet black hair and chestnut brown eyes. She was of average build and always looked good no matter what she wore. Kim had two children from her first marriage– a son and a daughter, who attended the local high school. Since they were stay-at-home moms, they frequently went to each other's homes to enjoy a cup of coffee. While Martha was on the quiet side, Kim had a larger-than-life personality and was not afraid to speak her mind. Kim had a way of bringing Martha out of her shell and making her feel that she mattered. The two women quickly became forever friends.

While Sam thoroughly enjoyed his job, it kept him on the road and away from home quite a bit. It was not unusual for Sam to be gone a week at a time, only to return late Friday and leave again early the following Monday. His only free time was the weekends. Because of this, Martha picked up doing more of the chores Sam previously had done, like mowing the yard and washing the car. She did this so Sam would spend time with her and the kids when he was home. Martha had never done yard work before, so learning how to use a lawn mower was new. Their home was sitting on three-quarters of an acre, so it took a good part of the day to maintain the yard. This yard was unlike the postage-stamp-sized yards Martha was used to in California. While doing yard work kept Martha in shape, it did leave her exhausted at the end of the day. She did all this while taking Nick to school and Jeremy to pre-school at a local church a few miles away. It was a busy time, but not so busy that Martha did not notice that she and Sam were growing apart. She quickly dismissed it as it being their season to raise the kids. There would be plenty of time for the two to spend together once the kids were grown.

Martha began finding receipts for jewelry Sam had purchased that she never received, which dashed her dreams. She asked Sam about it. He responded that someone had stolen the jewelry from his hotel room. Martha asked if he had reported it, and Sam quickly replied that he had not. Martha pressed on with her questions, and Sam finally snapped at her to let it go. This receipt was not the first time she had found evidence of jewelry purchased that she had never received. She let it go again, not wanting to imagine he was having an affair.

The distance between them grew. Sam continued to be gone, leaving for a week at a time, traveling throughout the South. When home, he hunkered down in his basement office with the door closed. From time to time, the kids would make their way down there to play quietly to be close to him. Once the kids were in bed, Martha would go downstairs to try and talk to Sam. He would ignore her, so she would go back upstairs to read or watch a little television. She usually went to bed around 10:00 pm. Sam would come upstairs around 1:00 in the morning. He would then wake her up and want sex. If Martha said she was too tired, he would start yelling profanity at her and he was not above using the "f" word repeatedly. He would even go so far as to threaten her that if she didn't comply, he would just go elsewhere to have sex. Sometimes he kept his voice low so the kids could not hear but there were many other times when she was afraid he would wake up the kids. She did not want them to hear the profanity and how he was speaking to their mother. Sam would even go to the extent to pick her up by her arms and shake her, like a rag doll, to wake her up. When she did comply with his request, which seemed like 99% of the time, she would just go through the motions. Sex was no longer enjoyable, and she considered it just another chore she had to do.

As time went on, so did Sam's verbal abuse. He would not come upstairs for dinner and eat with the rest of the family. When he would surface, he complained that the food was cold or didn't taste good. There were times he would throw the food, from the plate, across the room towards the kitchen sink. He didn't care where the food would land, and Martha was glad that he didn't throw the dishes and break them. One time he said that the food tasted so bad that he would rather eat his shoe. Martha found herself not knowing what to say or do. She was walking on eggshells as she didn't know what would set him off, and she wanted to keep the peace for the kids' sake.

One afternoon, Martha developed some pain in her mouth and went to the dentist. He told her that the three remaining wisdom teeth needed removal. Unfortunately, it meant she would be under anesthesia to perform the extractions. Sam arranged his schedule to take her to the dental office that morning, and they both returned home a couple of hours later. The procedure went well, and fortunately, Martha was fine. Seeing this, Sam told her to ensure the house received a special cleaning as his parents were coming up the next day. Martha was unaware her in-laws intended to visit, but she did a thorough cleaning that afternoon as requested. Besides her mouth being a bit tender, Martha was fine and went about her routine. A few days later, Sam left for the week. Martha observed she wasn't feeling well and sat down for a bit. Martha then went to get up and was so weak that she collapsed. Immediately, Martha called the dentist's office, who told her that she was experiencing the effects of the anesthesia and that it took several days to leave her system. Surprised at this, she did rest that afternoon and was better the next day. Martha mentioned this to Sam on his nightly call to her. He said it was no big deal. She was stunned at how calm he was with this news. It was as if he didn't care.

—

"Mom, are you still outside?" Rachel called.

Martha stared at her watch. Finally, it was getting time to wrap up the day. "Yes, Rachel, I'm coming in now!"

Once inside, she joined the kids at the dinner table and enjoyed a scoop of chocolate ice cream. There is nothing like seeing the smiles on kids' faces as they eat their ice cream. Next, Martha cleaned up the dishes from the dessert while Rachel tucked the kids into bed. Then, turning out the lights, Rachel told Martha goodnight.

"Tomorrow is another day," Martha mumbled. Then, she returned to her room to read a little and say her nighttime prayers, as she was grateful for so many things. Soon, Martha crawled into bed and was fast asleep.

CHAPTER 15

BEGINNING OF THE END

A couple of days passed before Martha met Liz at the park. She reminded Liz of the dinner invite for this coming Sunday. Liz accepted the invitation, and the two ladies spent the next few minutes watching the kids play on the jungle gym. Martha noticed that Liz appeared a bit tired. Her eyes had dark circles below them, and she just did not seem as energetic. 'I'm sure living in a hotel with kids is a bit challenging,' Martha speculated. She debated whether to say something but learned years ago that it is better not to make assumptions and ask questions. So instead, Martha took a more diplomatic route and asked, "How's the kitchen remodeling going, Liz?" She figured Liz would divulge more this way, and she would learn why Liz was so tired.

"It's coming along," Liz replied.

"That's great! Did the contractor give you a completion date for the kitchen?"

"Looks like another week or two."

Martha continued, not getting the answer she was hoping for, "Looking forward to Sunday. We plan to keep it simple with hamburgers and hot dogs."

"That sounds great." Liz and Martha sat in silence and concentrated on watching the kids play.

Unexpectedly, Liz began speaking. "Martha, do you remember when we first met, you told me to trust my gut?"

Martha turned to look and her. "Why, yes. Why do you ask?"

Liz looked. She did not want Martha to notice the tears welling up in her eyes. She paused for a minute before responding to Martha. "Last night was not a good night," Liz said. "Jeff returned to the hotel room last night in an awful mood. He then began throwing things and yelling at the kids. At one point, I worried he would take his anger out on Jess, but thankfully he didn't."

Martha's heart sunk. "That's horrible!" Martha inquires, "Liz, did you call 911?"

Liz shook her head, indicating that she did not make that call. "I did not, but I did think about it for a split second, but Jeff left the room to calm down. When he returned, he was calmer but quiet. He didn't look at or say anything to anyone. We all went to bed in silence."

"I will keep praying for you, Liz! It sounds like you are contemplating some life-changing decisions. Pray about it and seek guidance. That's all I can offer!"

Both women sat again in silence, focusing on the kids.

"Liz, you asked me a question," Martha says. "I'll answer that now." Liz looks at her, waiting expectantly for the response. "About nine months before I left Sam," Martha begins, "I purchased one of those national women's magazines at the grocery store checkout counter. The cover had an interesting recipe, and I was looking for something new to try. I didn't notice until I got home that the magazine had an article about recognizing signs of verbal abuse. I remember thinking, 'that's not for me,' I put the magazine down, not reading the article. A couple of days later, I picked up the magazine again and began to glance at the article. Well, I did more than just glance at the article. I read it. And then I read it a couple more times. 'This can't be true,' I muttered, not wanting to recognize the signs. I put the magazine back down. The next day, Sam came home from his week of traveling. I was standing in the kitchen when the sound of the garage door opening signaled that he was home. My stomach flipped – the same way it did the day I married Sam. I tried to shake off the feeling of not wanting to face this."

Sydney ran up to Martha and asked, "Grandma, can I have some water, please?"

Martha got the water out of her bag and handed it to Sydney. "Here you go, Sweetie."

Sydney spent a couple of minutes enjoying her water. Martha grabbed her water bottle and took some sips. Sydney finished her water and ran back to play with Jess and Amy. "Here I come," Sydney hollered. Martha and Liz chuckled.

Martha continued telling Liz her story. "I just remembered that I forgot to tell you about getting pneumonia. I got sick before reading the magazine article."

"You had pneumonia?" asks Liz.

"Yes, I did, and I ended up in the hospital for a few days. I remember that Jeremy caught pneumonia, and I took him to the pediatrician, who administered him two shots of antibiotics, one in each leg. The doctor looked at me as I was not feeling well and told me it appeared that I had pneumonia and should be checked out. I went home as I intended to care for Jeremy and Rachel. Sam and Nick were on a camping trip with the Boy Scouts and would be gone for a few days. However, I woke up in the middle of the night drenched. I realized I had a fever and did what I could to control it. I called Sam without delay. He answered, and after I asked him to come home because I was sick, he began yelling at me. 'How dare you call me with this! You deal with this. I am remaining here with Nick.'

I was so heartbroken that he didn't care about me enough to come home and take me to Urgent Care.

"The next morning, I reached out to my neighbor, Kim, who gladly babysat Rachel and Jeremy while I drove to the local hospital. They did all the blood work and x-rays of my lungs, and a nurse told me they needed to admit me. I was like, 'what did you say?' I told them I had under-aged kids with a neighbor and needed to get home. They did ask about my husband, and I told him that he was on a camping trip and could not to be disturbed. This nurse was not about to let me get my way to go home. She was firm with me and said fluid was in one lung and halfway up the other lung 'You are extremely sick,' I remember her saying. So, I relented and agreed to admission to the hospital. I called Kim in tears, telling her what was going on. She told me not to worry. I knew that the kids were safe with her.

"Once I was in my room, the doctor came to visit me. He stared at my chart and then confirmed the medications to which I am allergic. Since these medications are both antibiotics, he then asked me which one I could take. I told him, and he responded that I would receive the antibiotic intravenously, which would burn my arm. I didn't have a choice. I can only say that he wasn't kidding when he said it would burn. My arm was on fire. Not only that, but I also became very nauseous and couldn't keep anything down. It was not fun.

"On top of that, a nurse brought me paperwork to sign. I remember asking her about it, and she replied that it had to do with if I became unconscious and died. I peered at her and then said firmly, 'I am not going to die.' I signed the paperwork but trust me when I tell you that I did not intend to die. I do know that I prayed and prayed and prayed."

Liz interrupted, "And Sam was still camping?"

Martha replied and continued with her story. "After I settled in the room and signed all the paperwork, I called Sam and told him the doctor admitted me to the hospital. He agreed to come home, and he arranged with Kim to get the kids and take my car home from the hospital. The next morning, he did decide to visit me. Sam stayed for a few minutes, and his visit was more like he was checking to see if I was sick and, if so, how sick. The next few days were rough, but one morning, I woke up and was much better.

"The doctor came in and said, 'Welcome back!' I smiled and told him I had two questions – 'When can the I.V. be removed, and when can I go home?' I went home that afternoon. Sam didn't say much to me those first few days. I managed to keep the house straightened up and made simple meals. I rested in between as I needed to get my strength back. Sam did arrange his schedule to work from home the next few days, but he confined himself to his office downstairs, never asking how I was or if I needed anything."

"Nice guy," Liz said sarcastically.

Martha nodded in agreement and continued, "It took about a month for me to recover fully. I was amazed at how much pneumonia drains you, and how you quickly get tired. Fortunately, I recovered, but the tension and distance between Sam and I continued."

Liz glanced at the time and said she needed to get back. She called Amy and Jess to return, and Sydney came back with them as she was ready to go home too. Martha told Liz to come around 2:00 pm on Sunday.

As Sydney and Martha went home, Sydney commented that Amy was quieter than usual. "Really?" asked Martha. "Did Amy say something to you, Sydney?"

Sydney shook her head no. By this time, the two of them were home and grabbed some lunch. Sydney took a brief nap while Martha did a load of wash and checked on the roast in the crock pot for tonight's dinner.

Before she knew it, Sydney was up from her nap, in the family room playing with her toys, and the school bus dropped Sarah and Michael off as their school day was finished. 'Wow, this day went by quickly,' Martha observed.

Soon Rachel and James came home, and everyone was at the table enjoying their dinner. Rachel looked at Martha and said, "Mom, you look tired tonight. Did Sydney wear you out today?"

Martha chuckled and said, "Oh, no, not at all. I am feeling good."

Rachel was happy to hear this and told her mom to go relax as she would finish cleaning the kitchen and getting the kids to bed. Martha headed to the family room to do some crocheting. She had completed the afghan and was now making some small, crocheted pumpkins for fall. Martha liked keeping her hands busy. She finished the pumpkin she was making and headed upstairs for the night. Tomorrow would be another day!

CHAPTER 16

A TORNADO STRIKES

Sunday arrived without much fanfare. Martha, Rachel, James, and the kids went to Mass and then headed home to prepare for the afternoon get-together with Liz's family. Jeff, Liz, and the two kids arrived around 2:00 pm. They had stopped off at the local grocery store to bring some soft drinks, potato chips, and a veggie tray. Jess, Amy, and Sydney immediately went to the backyard to play. Jeff helped James with the BBQ while Liz, Rachel, and Martha completed meal preparations in the kitchen. Everyone was relaxed and having a wonderful time.

After everyone ate, James suggested they play a "Go Fish" game with the kids. Sarah won the first-round while Jess, assisted by Liz, won the second round. Rachel brought the ice cream out for dessert, and everyone ate their ice cream cones in the backyard. It appeared to Martha that Jeff and Liz were enjoying the afternoon away from the hotel and the stress that living in cramped quarters with two kids brings. All appeared fine on the surface! Finally, Jeff looked at his watch and told everyone it is time to go. Jeff and Liz express their thanks and appreciation for the afternoon of fun. Liz asked Martha if she would be back at the park tomorrow, and Martha said that she would.

Later that night, Rachel and Martha sat on the front porch discussing the day's events. They both agreed it was a fantastic day – great food and company. Martha secretly hoped that today's get-together was what Jeff needed, but thought, 'time will tell!'

Rachel excused herself to get the kids ready for bed. Martha stayed outside a little longer as it was just dark enough to see the stars. She found the big dipper and spotted a shooting star and made a wish. It was getting late, so she went in and said goodnight to everyone. She went to her room, got ready for bed, and turned out the light.

Knock! Knock! Martha heard the raps of little hands tapping on her door.

"Grandma are you awake?" asked Michael.

"No, I'm not," Martha replied. She rolled over to her other side, secretly hoping Michael would try his parent's door.

But he didn't and knocked again. "Grandma, I'm hungry," Michael said.

"Ok, Michael, give me a minute, and I'll come downstairs," Martha replied.

"Yesssss!" Michael yells as he runs down the stairs as if to wake the dead.

Martha soon follows him downstairs and begins making pancakes. He got the first two pancakes that came right off the griddle. The grin on his face was a sight to behold, and Martha was chuckling. 'What a cutie!' Martha commented to herself.

A couple of minutes later, the others come downstairs, dressed, and ready for breakfast. The organized chaos of the morning routine had begun with breakfast, packed lunches, backpack checks for Sarah and Michael, school bus honking, and Rachel and James off to work. 'Whew!' Martha muttered. 'Another morning off to a good start!'

Martha went upstairs to finish dressing. When she returned downstairs, she found Sydney holding the bag Martha takes to the park. "Well, what do you have there? If I didn't know any better, that looks like the bag we take to the park?"

Sydney laughed and then asked if they could go.

"Sure thing, Sydney! Let's go," Martha says with a big grin on her face.

Martha and Sydney arrived at the park, and before Sydney can go to the jungle gym, Martha coats her down with sunblock.

"Thank you, Grandma!" Sydney says as she runs away to play.

Martha sat on the bench and took out a book to read. The same book she had been trying to read since before she met Liz. Since meeting Liz, there had not been the opportunity to catch up on reading as the two ladies always seemed to find something to discuss. Martha began reading, and Liz arrives with Jess and Amy about fifteen minutes later. Liz told her kids to go and play after she put sunblock on them and then sat down next to Martha.

Liz was smiling today and thanked Martha for their wonderful time yesterday.

"Good, I am so glad that everyone enjoyed themselves. It was a wonderful day!" Martha retorted. "How was Jeff last night? It seems like he had a fun time and was relaxed?"

Liz said things were much better, and the two talked about what had happened. Liz continued and said that Jeff expressed remorse about the incident.

"Hmm," Martha replies.

"You don't think this is a good sign?"

"It's not up to me," Martha states. "It's about what you think, Liz."

Liz looked at Martha, hoping she would say more, but she remained quiet. Liz then asked Martha if she ever sought psychiatric help. Martha acknowledged that she had, and Liz asked Martha to tell her about her involvement in seeing a psychiatrist.

Martha responded, "The last time we spoke, I told you about getting pneumonia and how Sam and I grew further apart. One day, while Nick and Jeremy were at school, I called my mom. As I already had my monthly allotted call, I was hoping Sam would not find out about this extra call. Fortunately, she answered the phone, and I told her I was not happy but didn't know why. I remember crying and starting to tell her a few things. She said, 'I have been praying for years for this call.' I was shocked, and when I asked her to explain, she replied, 'Your dad and I would see how controlling Sam and his family were. Sam has been pulling you away from us for years. We recognized we had to be patient and wait.' My mom then suggested I seek professional help. I found a psychiatrist and was able to see Dr. Jones, a psychiatrist, on the mornings that Rachel attended preschool."

"Did you tell Sam you were seeing a psychiatrist?"

"Heck no! He would have found every reason in the book, including calling psychiatrists' quacks, to prevent me from seeing the doctor. I will never forget my first visit with Dr. Jones. I started writing down every thought and feeling I could remember to prepare for the visit. I walked into Dr. Jones' office with pages and pages. I began reading what I wrote as he sat silently for the next forty-five minutes. When my time was up, I said, 'I don't understand what is wrong with me.' His reply, 'There is nothing wrong with you.' As I was driving to go and pick up Rachel from preschool, it suddenly dawned on me, 'If there is nothing wrong with me, then why do I feel so awful?'"

Martha stopped talking when she saw Sydney running up towards her. Sydney dug into the bag to get her water, took some sips, and headed back out to play.

Martha told Liz that Dr. Jones treated her for the next several months, where she learned about codependency and needing to draw boundaries.

"At one session," Martha continued, "Dr. Jones said, 'Something happened to you when you were about five or six that has impacted your codependency.' I was shocked. After the visit, I went downstairs to the payphone in the lobby, called my mom, and told her what Dr. Jones said. Her response was, 'Oh!' Shocked. I asked her what had happened. She told me that was the time my grandparents were divorcing. I replied that I recalled that, but my mom indicated there was more to this and told me about an incident I didn't know. My dad went to my grandparent's house as my grandfather had pulled a gun on my grandmother. I'm not sure of all the details, but my mom would say that my dad was distraught and that I must have sensed it, even though they did their best to shield my sister and me from the incident. I was stunned. I had no idea of these family dynamics."

Martha reached for her water and drank some sips. She told Liz that she wanted to share another incident involving Sam and his disregard for his family's welfare, so Martha continued, "One day, Sam comes upstairs and informs me that a bad thunderstorm, possibly with tornadoes, would be hitting our area later that night. He said he would soon leave to head out before the storm."

"What? He was leaving the family when danger was coming?" asked Liz, shocked by Martha's words.

Martha continued, "Yes, that's right. He left us to fend for ourselves. I had been through tornados and hurricanes before and knew we had the needed food, water, and battery supplies."

Liz added, "Don't forget, you've dealt with earthquakes too!"

Martha chuckled, "Let's say I deeply respect Mother Nature. Later that night, I made the decision that we would spend the night downstairs in the basement for added protection. I made the downstairs couch into a bed where Rachel and I slept while the boys slept on the floor in sleeping bags. I made light of it and told them to pretend it was a camping adventure.

Around two in the morning, I awoke to the train sound. I froze in the bed as I recognized that sound meant a tornado was hitting us. I quickly glanced at the kids who were peacefully sleeping. I debated whether I should wake them. Should I wake them up so they are fully aware that the tornado could directly hit us? Do I want them to be scared? Panic? Become hysterical? Do I want to see that fear in their faces? Or is it better that they sleep in peace and not know what hit them should the tornado directly hit us? These questions raced through my head as I looked at each of them individually as they slept. All I know is that I didn't want to survive this if it meant that my kids perished. I didn't know what to do so I began to pray. I asked God that whatever His will was for us, all I ask is that we are kept together – dead or alive. The next thing I remember was waking up the following day to the telephone ringing. I answered the phone, and it was a neighbor checking on us to see if we had sustained damage. I responded that I didn't know as I had just woken up. I was totally taken back that I had fallen asleep with the tornado so close, but I instantly realized that God had protected us.

"By that time, the kids were waking up, and we went upstairs. Everything inside the house was intact – no broken windows, the roof had not collapsed or blown off, and everything inside was dry. I quickly got dressed to check on the outside. Our neighborhood was a forest of trees – large oak and pine trees scattered with flowering dogwood trees dispersed in between. The lots were cleared just enough to contain a house and yard and the developer made a point to retain the vast number of these large trees in this community. However, with all these trees, I was concerned some had blown down in this storm. And I was right. Two large oak trees, about one hundred feet in height, had blown over in the side yard, but thankfully, didn't come near the house. I found a few roof shingles blown off, and the kids' playhouse had blown into Kim's yard across the street. Her home had a huge pine tree limb, about fifty feet long and nine inches wide, blow into the roof as if a javelin player had thrown it. Another neighbor down the street also had a large pine tree fall, significantly damaging the house's right side. I was so lucky and appreciated God blessing and protecting us that night.

"I went back inside, and the phone rang again. This time it was Sam checking in. I told him that a tornado had hit, and he should come home and bring a chain saw. Instead, Sam started yelling at me. I was not in the mood, so I repeated that he needed to come home and bring a chain saw, and I hung up. I could not believe he was yelling at me. I just went through a life and death situation, not just my life, also the lives of each one of the kids. I did the best I could to protect the kids and all he does is yell at me. How was this even possible? Who does this? If anything, he should have been the one apologizing that he even left to begin with. He abandoned us, his family, when we needed him the most. I was sad that he had no regard for us but the more I thought about it, the sadness turned into anger. When did he become so callous? When did all the hopes and dreams we once had for our future, to include kids and a family, go by the wayside? When did he become the person I no longer recognized? Or was it always there and I never saw his true colors until now?"

Liz stared at Martha, stunned. "I am so sorry, Martha! How scary!"

"It's okay, Liz, it happened so long ago, and I have moved on." Looking at her watch, Martha told Liz she needed to leave and would continue her story tomorrow. In the meantime, she told Liz not to be afraid to solicit additional help. Finally, Martha informed Sydney it is time to go, and they head home.

After dinner, Martha retreated to the front porch. Rachel soon joined her and asked Martha about her day. Martha told her that she told Liz about the tornado that happened all those years ago. Rachel reached out for her mom's hand and gently squeezed it. They sat there for a few moments, in silence, looking at the stars in the night's sky.

CHAPTER 17

SUICIDE ATTEMPT

The following day, Sydney complained she had a sore throat. Martha kept her in and ensured she had some chicken soup and plenty of liquids to fend off a potential cold. A couple of days passed, and with Sydney feeling her usual rambunctious self, Martha took her to the park. They saw Liz, and Amy ran up to Sydney, hugging her. Amy told Sydney that she had missed her. Martha explained that Sydney was a bit under the weather but was fine, and the kids ran off to play.

Martha looked at Liz, whose huge smile looked like she was bursting at the seams to tell Martha something. Martha couldn't resist and took the bait. "Liz, you are beaming; what is going on?"

Liz told her that her kitchen remodel would be done by the end of the week. She couldn't wait to get back and have her kitchen again.

"That's wonderful news!" Martha exclaimed and then jokingly asked, "When are we coming for dinner?"

Liz smiles and promises that it will be soon.

"Martha," Liz said softly, "Do you mind continuing your story? I know you went through a lot, but I find your story fascinating and admire your strength in dealing with all of this."

"I don't mind telling more, but I warn you, the worst part is coming up."

"Ok, Martha," Liz responded.

"Let's see," Martha began, "where I last left off was telling you about the tornado. About a week later, after the kids were in bed, I went downstairs to Sam and asked to speak with him. He agreed but continued working as I tried to talk. I told him that I wasn't happy. Sam replied that my happiness was on me, and he wasn't responsible for it. I told him that I wasn't happy with this marriage and that this was a joint problem. Sam was stunned, 'What do you mean you are not happy in this marriage?' 'You heard me. I am not happy, and I want a divorce.' I was waiting for him to blow his top, but he didn't. Instead, he just stared at me. I take that back; he was glaring at me. With nothing more to say, I went upstairs to bed. He soon followed me upstairs while I climbed into bed. He sat down in the beige leather reclining chair that was situated near our bedroom's bay window. The chair would squeak with any turn or movement from whomever was sitting in it. The room was dark with the only light coming from a small plugged-in night light from across the room. I could feel the weight of his stare at me while I tried to sleep. His face was expressionless. His eyes just focused straight on me.

"Knowing there were guns in the house, I listened for the squeak of the chair which meant he was moving, and, if his movement meant he was just repositioning himself in the chair or getting up out of the chair. I feared he might, at any time, go downstairs to get a gun and do something awful. I fathomed that if he moved out of that chair, I would call the police. All kinds of thoughts crossed my mind. Was he going to kill me? Would he kill the kids? Should I be afraid? What was he thinking? My mind couldn't shut off, so I prayed. Prayer gave me some peace, but I tossed and turned all night. Periodically I raised my head to see if he was sleeping in the chair. He wasn't. He just kept staring at me with no expression on his face.

"I didn't sleep much that night. The next morning, he was still sitting in the chair. I asked him if he had gotten any sleep, and he responded that he had not. Then I told him that I was concerned he would go downstairs for a gun. He admitted that the idea crossed his mind. I left the room to get the kids ready for school and thanked God that we were safe."

"Oh my God," Liz exclaimed. "I can't believe this! He was thinking of using a gun?"

Martha took a minute or two to grab some water to drink. When she heard herself tell this story to Liz, she substantiated just how dangerous the situation had been, and thanked God nothing had happened.

Martha continued, "Yes, it was pretty bad. My emotional well-being was quickly deteriorating. I spoke with Dr. Jones about this, who prescribed an antidepressant and Xanax for sleep. I was quickly heading towards having major depression."

Liz spotted Jess running towards her. He asked for a snack and some water. Liz and Martha asked him how he was enjoying the jungle gym. He shook his head affirmatively and smiled a huge grin. Jess's vocabulary was limited, but Liz worked with him to get him to speak more.

Jess went back to play, and Martha began again. "Although the doctor prescribed the medication, the situation at home worsened, and not long after, I began having suicidal thoughts and thinking of ways to end my life. I remember thinking that the kids would be better off without me and that my life was useless. One night, after the kids were in bed and Sam was still working downstairs, I took several of the Xanax pills. The ironic thing is that I don't swallow pills, so this was very out of character for me."

Martha looked at Liz and sees tears in her eyes. "I can't believe things got that bad for you. I'm so sorry," Liz said.

Martha stopped talking and reached down for her water. She needed to regain her composure so she could continue.

"Wait!" exclaimed Liz. "Doesn't God frown on suicide?"

"Yes, He does," Martha replied. "For the Church, suicide is a mortal sin.

The suicide attempt is not something I am proud of, but I was at the end of my rope, and as I learned later during therapy sessions that it is one of the negative side effects of living with a narcissistic gaslighter. I was unaware of narcissism, much less gaslighting, so learning about these terms in the therapy sessions and how I was impacted, helped me to heal. It was very liberating to know the truth and that I was not crazy as Sam kept telling me."

"Did you leave a note? What did it say?"

"That's a great question," Martha replied. "In all honesty, I purposely did not write a note. I wanted people to realize that Sam did this to me – he drove me to my breaking point. By this time, I was in a downhill spiral of negative thoughts that would not stop and the only relief I saw from this spiral was suicide. What were some of those thoughts? Well, I thought I was useless. I was worthless. I was unlovable. I had nothing to live for. My kids would be better off without me. Heck, I couldn't even get out of bed. I didn't want to do anything. I had no joy. I didn't want to see anyone, including my children. I was weighed down with the world as I knew it. I did not like this world and I wanted out.

"Sam did not understand, or even want to understand, what was going on with me. He just continued to add to my downhill spiral with his continual words of how lazy and worthless I was. Looking back, I was angry, lashing out, and desperate for help, and I didn't know who to go to or how to get that help. After taking the last pill, I prayed to God that he would forgive me. I remember saying, 'Please forgive me' over and over repeatedly.

"The next thing I remember was waking up in the hospital. A nurse came in and asked if I knew where I was. I said 'no'.

"She explained that I tried to take my life and that I was being held for seventy-two hours for observation. Memory of those pills came back to me. I asked her how long I had been at the hospital, and she replied that it had been about twelve hours. I quickly calculated the time when I took the pills and the current time which was a total of twenty-four hours since I swallowed the pills. The nurse further conveyed that my stomach was not pumped as too much time had elapsed from the time I had taken the pills to when I was brought into the hospital. In other words, hours went by before Sam or the kids noticed there was something wrong. Another indication to me that he didn't love me.

A couple of hours later from my conversation with the nurse, Dr. Jones came to visit. He told me, 'Your environment is making you sick.' He was never a man known for saying a lot of words but when he did speak, they packed a punch. I nodded in agreement. Dr. Jones did say that he was prescribing some different medication for the depression, and it would take a couple of weeks before I would be feeling better. He explained that my serotonin levels, which regulate one's mood, would need to stabilize. Knowing I had another forty-eight hours in the hospital, I began to contemplate my next move.

One thing was for sure was that I could not go back to that house, or at least go back with Sam in it. I asked a nurse for some paper and pen so I could make a list of what it would take to end the marriage. I knew I needed to find a place to live and get a job – one with health benefits. I hoped that being a stay-at-home mom for all these years wouldn't make it too difficult to find work. It also meant that I needed to put a resume together. In addition to all of this, I would need to find a divorce attorney. I added creating a preliminary budget to the list but without knowing how much rent would be and what type of job I could get along with salary amount, a budget would be hard. All I could do was create line items, like rent, clothes, insurance, car payment, etc. for the budget. As the list grew, I became overwhelmed and put it down to get some rest.

"Late that afternoon, my mom and sister came to visit. To my surprise,

Sam had called them, and they immediately flew out. I told them I needed to file for divorce and why I needed to do so, and they agreed with the decision. Sam came to visit me while my mom and sister watched the kids. I informed him of my decision but that we would have to figure out how to co-exist as I needed distance from him. He agreed that I could return home and when I was at the house, he would be in North Carolina. If he needed something, he agreed to contact me when he would be there so I would have my choice of either being there when he arrived or being absent from the house.

"The next couple of weeks were not only busy with my own healing but with finding work, an apartment, and an attorney. Having a plan in place seem to focus and energize me. While I had some sadness that the marriage was ending, for the first time, in many years, the future looked bright and very promising. It was good to be alive! Both Sam and I found divorce attorneys and, within a couple of meetings, agreed upon the distribution of the marital assets. The biggest question that remained was custody of Nick. Because of Nick's age at the time, the state provided him the option to choose where to reside. He chose his dad, as I perceived he would. Knowing he was Sam's favorite, Nick figured he would get what he wanted. Jeremy and Rachel would come with me. When it came time for me to leave the house, Sam yelled his infamous words, 'You will never make it, and no one will ever love you.'"

The two women sat quietly for a long while. Martha said that this all happened long ago and that she is not the same person she was then.

"Leaving Sam was the best gift I ever awarded myself," Martha said. "For the first time, I could breathe, which was exhilarating. I had challenges ahead of me to face still, but I was determined never to let anyone have control over me again. And I was even more determined to end this cycle of abuse. I did not want my kids to be victims or victimizers of abuse and vowed I would spend the rest of my life doing what I needed to honor this pledge."

Liz glanced at Martha while she was saying this and saw Martha's jaw tighten, giving her a fierce look of determination on her face. She knew that Martha meant every word and saw, for the first time, that nothing would stop Martha from protecting her children. Liz gained a new respect for Martha, as the phoenix who rose from the ashes.

"Well, that's certainly enough storytelling for today," Martha said interrupting the silence. "I'll see you back here tomorrow. And I am so happy to hear about your kitchen. Please bring some pictures – I would love to see it."

Liz smiled at Martha and hugged her goodbye. This was the first time the two women hugged, and they both needed the connection. Liz didn't feel alone in her situation, and Martha felt safe sharing her story, hoping that it would help Liz. Finally, Martha and Sydney return home.

CHAPTER 18

JOINT CUSTODY

A few days passed before Martha and Sydney returned to the park. The weather had been very windy, and since Martha wore contact lenses, she avoided environments where debris would quickly get into her eyes. Unfortunately, these windy conditions also created poor air quality as they had a way of kicking up dust and significantly reducing visibility. Fortunately, these conditions don't often occur in the desert.

Liz, Jess, and Amy greeted Martha and Sydney upon reaching the park. The kids went off to play, and Martha observed Liz's happiness.

"How's the new kitchen?" Martha asked.

"It's wonderful," replied Liz. "All state-of-the-art appliances, new white cabinets, counter tile, and the backsplash is marble with gray colored veins meandering through the marble. I cooked my first dinner the other night. It feels good to be out of the hotel and back to normal."

Martha smiled and told her that all sounded fantastic. She then asked, "What was the first meal you cooked in your new kitchen?"

"That's easy," Liz responded. "Beef Stroganoff."

Martha told Liz that was one of her favorite meals. Jess comes ran up asking for some water which Liz provided. He then went back to play with the others.

"Liz," Martha began, "How are things with Jeff?"

"Things are good right now," replied Liz.

"That's good to hear,"

The two women sat silently for a few minutes, watching the kids play. The weather was a little cooler than it had been, but with the sun out, the air was warm. Finally, Liz turned to Martha and asked, "Martha, did your life get easier once you left Sam?"

Martha paused for a minute and then responded, "It took a while."

Liz questioned her on why it took a while.

Martha replied, "In one word – visitation. The divorce cost a lot of money as it entailed obtaining the divorce decree and child support and custody agreements. Sam did not think he had to follow the divorce decree even though it was a legally binding document recorded in the County Clerk's Office. I agreed to forfeit alimony in exchange for Sam assuming the credit card debt, which, for the most part, were items he charged. I also accepted a lower child support payment to offset the funds needed for Nick. I never wanted Sam to tell Nick I didn't contribute to his well-being. However, when it came to visitation, Sam only wanted the kids when he wanted them. Sam ignored the agreed-upon schedule. If I told him the day he wanted that week didn't work for me, he would yell and scream and then threaten he was going to take the kids away from me permanently and that I would never see them again. He did this quite often. I found myself giving in all the time. To top it all off, Sam would tell me that Nick didn't want to see me. I asked to hear those words from Nick himself, and Sam refused. I feared that Nick was now under the same verbal abuse I had escaped, and my heart broke.

"About a year after the divorce, I met a gentleman, John, who lived in a different city a couple of hours away. He was an attorney. John and I met through work; at first, it just entailed conversations over the phone. One evening as we talked, Sam came to my home and started loudly banging on the door. I did open the door, and he demanded to see the kids. Mind you, it was not his day for visitation, and it was late and nearing their bedtime. Sam yelled at me, barged open the door, and came in. My friend indicated he was going to contact the police. When the police pulled up around the corner, Sam immediately left. I filed a police report, but the police told me there was nothing they would do, even after I told them my story and my fear for the children's safety. After the police left, I called John and told him what the police said. He advised that I move further away from Sam and put more distance between us."

Martha stopped when she saw Amy coming toward them. She wanted a hug from Liz, and the two cuddled for a couple of minutes. Liz gave her some water, and Amy returned to the playground.

Martha continued her story, "The idea of moving was enticing, especially when a second incident with the police occurred."

"What happened?" Liz asked.

Martha began, "During the summer, Sam had the kids for six weeks straight. Being separated from them for this long was extremely hard for me. I could pick them up for dinner on Wednesday nights, which I did. When I took them back, on this particular Wednesday, Jeremy and Rachel began crying and saying they didn't want to go. I asked what was happening, and their response indicated they were being touched inappropriately. When I arrived at Sam's home, I went to the door with the kids and told Sam to pack up their things because they didn't want to return. He blew up at me. He yanked Jeremy into the house so hard that I worried he had dislocated Jeremy's shoulder, and then he grabbed Rachel out of my arms. I called the police. I waited outside until they came and filled me in. They told me there was nothing they could do, even after I reported how he had treated Jeremy and the comments made at dinner.

"I now recognized I needed to put some more distance between Sam and me. John suggested moving closer to him, which was a definite idea, but I had only seen him in person a couple of times, and the kids had never met him. I didn't want to confuse Jeremy and Rachel more than they already were, especially since Sam was seeing his lover regularly, and all three kids were very aware of this.

"So, when the school year finished, I moved closer to John. I rented a small home for Jeremy, Rachel, and myself. Sam was always worried that I would move back to California as he understood that was where my family was. So, while he always threatened to take away the kids, I wasn't moving out of state unless all three kids were with me. I did not want to separate the kids any further. It was hard on me, but it was my way of letting Nick know I was not abandoning him."

"Did moving away help the situation?" asked Liz.

"Yes and no," replied Martha. "Yes, in that, Sam began to visit the kids less and less, which helped me try and stabilize them. No, in that, when he did visit the kids, he learned how to play the 'Ice Cream Daddy' by purchasing them toys and then constantly berating me to them. He was not above using profanity to describe me. So, when the kids returned, it took me almost a week to undo the damage Sam did during the visit. It pained me to see the kids now being Sam's target of abuse. I did begin to wonder if I had made the right decision. These thoughts crossed my mind a couple of times. When they did, I prayed and called my mom, who assured me that I had made the right decision, that this would pass, and that Sam didn't want the kids. I understood this more as time went on."

Always curious to hear more, Liz asked Martha about her relationship with John.

Martha responded, "After the move, I did introduce the kids to John. However, Jeremy was not handling the divorce or visitation well and was becoming increasingly angry. Juggling a job, a new relationship, and raising two kids, was getting a bit much, especially after realizing that Jeremy was not going to accept anyone else in my life, so I ended the relationship and moved back to California."

Martha glanced at the time and said she had to go. She teased Liz about an invite for dinner to see the new kitchen and agreed to a get-together this coming weekend. Then she and Sydney headed home.

That afternoon was quiet for Martha, and dinner was uneventful. After dinner, Martha went out to the front porch to finish watching the sun set behind the mountains. She reflected on the day's conversation and was so proud of herself that she didn't give up and persevered through those tough days. Her family was much better off for it. Smiling, Martha went upstairs to read a bit before calling it a day.

CHAPTER 19

THE GET-AWAY

The following day, Martha woke up and realized she had slept later than usual 5:00 am wake-up time. Going downstairs, she heard the clatter of the dishes being cleared from the table and put into the dishwasher.

James saw her and said, "Good morning, sleepyhead!"

Martha laughed and told him good morning. Sarah and Michael rush right by her to get out the door as the school bus honked, ready to take them to school. She told them to have a wonderful day! Headed to the kitchen to get a cup of coffee, Martha saw Rachel and kissed her.

"Mom, are you feeling okay?" asked Rachel.

"Yes," replied Martha, a little irritated that she couldn't sleep in occasionally.

Sensing Martha's irritation, Rachel offered her breakfast and took off to finish getting ready for work.

Martha sat at the table and looked Sydney, who gave her a big smile. "Good morning, Syd," Martha said lovingly. "Want to go to the park today?

Sydney shook her head, yes. After completing their morning routine, they headed to the park to their familiar spot.

Seeing Liz and her kids, Sydney ran ahead of Martha and greeted them. Martha caught up and said hello. Both Liz and Martha put sunblock on the kids, and they ran off to play.

"What a morning," Martha exclaimed.

"Why, what happened?" Liz asked.

Chuckling, Martha told her she overslept as if that had been a sin for not helping out with the morning routine. "Oh well, I'll get over it," Martha chuckled.

"We all have those mornings once in a while," Liz said as she tried to comfort Martha.

"Darn it!" Martha said. "I completely forgot to tell Rachel about your invite for this Sunday. I will text her about it now so she can get it on her calendar. I can't wait to see your new kitchen!"

Liz watched Martha text Rachel about Sunday's dinner. A couple of minutes later, Rachel replied Martha told her that it is a definite go for Sunday, and Liz smiled.

Martha turned to Liz and asked if she wanted to hear more about her story.

"You know I do, Martha," replied Liz.

"Well, okay then. I believe I ended this story with us moving to California, but I need to back up a bit. As I said, there were issues with the kids and the visits with their dad. After I moved a few hours away, the visits became fewer. It was clearer that he didn't want the kids and used them to control me. I decided to go back to Church as I recognized that my healing had to start with me doing the right thing. Growing up on the Baltimore Catechism, I saw Church more as a set of rules to be followed. The divorce taught me faith is truly about the relationship with God through His Son, Jesus.

"When I flipped that switch, I acknowledged I needed to repair the damage I had caused to my relationship with Jesus. Yes, I know He died on the cross for my sins, but I wasn't doing my part to strive to be the person

He created me to be. That needed to change. I began with having Jeremy and Rachel baptized Catholic and followed up with them receiving First Confession and First Holy Communion. These are especially important and significant sacraments the Church practices, and I wanted them to be part of this. I had hoped that this would help with Jeremy's anger issues but, sadly, it didn't. My boss, a successful general contractor, and a devout Christian would pray and read Scripture in the office. One day, when I was alone in the office working, the words, 'plans for you!' were whispered into my left ear. Startled, I got up and walked around the office because I worried someone was inside as the voice came directly from behind me. Later that night, I told a friend about this, and she said to look up Jeremiah 29:11. I did, and it read, 'For I know well the plans I have in mind for you, says the LORD, plans for your welfare, not for woe! Plans to give you a future full of hope.'[4] After reading this, tears streamed down my face. He had this. All I needed to do was to keep the faith. I had such hope and peace that night."

Looking at Liz, Martha could see the shocked look on her face.

"That's incredible, Martha," Liz said.

Both women stared at each other, and tears formed in their eyes. They stayed silent for a few moments. Martha took that time to thank God for that understanding and reminding her that He was still in control.

Then, Martha returned to telling her story, "Around this time, Nick was getting ready to graduate from high school. He had been accepted to several universities and selected one where there would be some distance from his dad. I knew he needed to get out of that house.

"After Nick's graduation, Sam married his mistress. The surprising thing about this was that he did not invite any of the kids. But then again, none of the kids liked her. The icing on the cake was that Sam moved to

4   Holy Bible, The New American Bible, World Publishing, 1970

another state with his new wife. That meant the time was right for me to move back home to California."

"You could have moved at any time back to California, right?" asked Liz.

Martha replied, "Yes, that is true. There is a federal law that allows it, and this law is part of the Interstate Commerce Act. The lawyer tried to explain it to me. Still, I was insistent that the divorce decree contained language that I had the right to relocate back to California. I wanted Sam to acknowledge it, and sign that he understood this. I may have had the law on my side, but I wanted additional protection in the decree. It was better with Nick out of Sam's house and away at school. Sam would have less influence over him which would give Nick the time to heal. I was also careful as I didn't want Sam to ever tell the kids that I took them away from him. He moved out of state first, so he couldn't use that excuse. I was ecstatic!"

Jess came up to Liz and asked for some water. He struggled to say the words correctly, so Liz spent a few moments with him to work on his pronunciation. After a few moments, Jess mastered his request for water and drank happily from the water bottle.

"So, how did you get to California? Did you fly there with the kids?" asked Liz.

"Well, I sold what I could, had movers get the rest of the items, and then drove three thousand miles across the country with the two kids in the car. We got in the car at sunrise and stopped at sunset. It was a long haul but so worth it. Jeremy and Rachel were so good spending all that time in the car. They had some video games which kept them busy, and I made sure we stopped every two hours. I also used this as an educational opportunity as we traveled through each state. But let me tell you, I was so happy when I pulled into my parent's driveway as that would be where we would spend the next couple of weeks. Several years had passed since the divorce, but I was finally home."

Martha glanced at her watch and told Liz it was time for her to go home with Sydney. As they left, Martha told Liz that she would see them all on Sunday.

CHAPTER 20

NICK'S ADVENTURES

Sunday had arrived - the day Martha and her family were invited over to Liz's house. Rachel and Martha were anxious to see the new kitchen. Rachel was contemplating remodeling her kitchen and wanted to see Liz's color schemes and the chosen appliances. Sydney was excited as it was another chance to see her friends, Jess and Amy. Martha had made a macaroni salad the night before, and Rachel stopped after church to pick up some drinks. Then, with everyone piled into the car, Martha's family left to go to Liz's home.

Upon arriving, Amy opened the door and welcomed everyone. Jeff and Liz came downstairs with Liz holding Jess in her arms. Liz took them to the kitchen and proudly showed off her new kitchen. It was beautiful. The white, shaker-styled cabinets had beautiful oblong stainless handles, with some cabinets having glass panels highlighting some beautiful Waterford China pieces. Liz had added an oversized farmhouse kitchen sink that fit nicely with the cabinets and countertops. The kitchen's highlight was white granite countertops with random gray swirls. Martha had never seen anything like it.

"Gorgeous!" Martha told Liz.

Rachel was admiring the kitchen appliances – all state of the art with the latest cooking options, including an oversized refrigerator built into the cabinets. "I could live in this kitchen," remarked Rachel. Everyone laughed, and James jokingly told Rachel not to get any ideas.

Jeff, James, and the kids went outside while Liz, Rachel, and Martha remained inside the kitchen. The ladies got busy with dinner preparations, and soon it was time to sit down and eat in the backyard, which was perfect for outdoor entertainment. There was an oversized barbeque within a large countertop area with a sink and small refrigerator. All along the patio's perimeter were small sitting areas with either a fire pit or a propane gas heater nearby. The adults sat down at the outside dining table that seated six. Jeff had set up another small table with chairs for the five kids. Jeff and James cooked the steaks and chicken breasts, and with Martha's macaroni salad, Liz's mac and cheese salad, and a house salad, there was more than enough to eat. Liz brought out a chocolate cake for dessert. Everyone was having fun; before they knew it, it was time to say goodnight.

Rachel perceived James was quiet on the ride home and asked him about it. He shrugged it off. After arriving home, the kids went inside, and James asked Rachel and Martha to stay behind for a minute. Once the kids got far away, James told Martha he did not feel good about Jeff.

"Why do you say that?" asked Martha.

"I can't put my finger on it," replied Jeff, "but I didn't get a good vibe from Jeff tonight. Please be careful, Martha."

She shook her head in agreement.

The next day, the ladies met up in the park again, and the kids went off to play on the slides and jungle gym. Martha thanked Liz again for the fantastic dinner and complimented her on the beautiful kitchen.

"Sometimes, we must go through challenges before we see the blessings," Martha said, and Liz agreed.

"Martha, you left off your story with driving to California. What happened next?" Liz inquired.

"Did I tell you all about Nick's graduation? Martha asked.

"No," Liz said, "what happened?"

Martha began, "Nick was preparing to graduate from high school. I hardly visited or spoke with him, which strained our relationship. He always had an excuse. I remember asking him what his plans were for graduation. He asked me not to come for fear of his father's reaction. Nick was getting the same barrage of negative and derogatory comments about me that Jeremy and Rachel had also shared. While Nick wouldn't say it, these comments bothered him. I kept quiet and did not indicate to him that I was coming. I went to the high school directly, explained the situation, and got tickets to attend. My mom and sister flew out from California to go with the kids and me. They did not want me facing Sam alone."

Martha stopped talking when Sydney ran up to her, crying. "What happened, Sydney?"

Sobbing, Sydney told her she fell and scraped her knee. Martha picked her up and put her on her lap. Martha grabbed a sanitizing wipe out of her bag and cleaned the area. It was a tiny scrape, and Martha kissed it all better.

Sydney took off, running back to the jungle gym. Martha smiled. "I wish our boo-boos would go away with a couple of kisses!" Martha exclaimed.

Liz affirmatively shook her head in agreement.

"What happened at the graduation?" Liz asked. "Oh yes, well, we all arrive and find a seat. Since several hundred kids were graduating, the school used the football stadium for the graduation ceremony. And, as you can imagine, there are several hundred seats to choose where to sit. Wouldn't you know, but Sam and his family came and sat down three rows ahead of us. My sister and I stared at each other. I know my eyes were wide open with shock. Mary told me to keep calm and that it will be all right. I have the worst luck, which is why, Liz, I don't go to Vegas. My luck stinks!"

Liz burst out laughing.

"At any rate," Martha continued, "Sam did not know I was there until Nick walked across the stage to get his diploma. That is when my mom, sister, Jeremy, Rachel, and I began clapping hard and cheering him on. Sam turned around and saw us, rolled his eyes, and turned back towards the stage. He and his family did not clap or cheer for Nick. Sam saw that Jeremy and Rachel were there but never said anything, not even hello."

"Unbelievable!" Liz exclaimed.

"Right?" Martha quipped and continued. "My sister and I left our seats to get down to the football field to find Nick. With several hundred graduates, it was a sea of white caps and gowns, and looking for Nick was like looking for a needle in a haystack. My mom followed behind with Jeremy and Rachel. Mary and I wanted to get to Nick before Sam did, and we were successful. We called Nick's name. As soon as he saw us, he froze in his tracks, and a look of terror struck his face. I told him everything was going to be okay. Nick said that Sam and his grandparents were here and were surprised when I told him we'd already seen them. Nick constantly glanced around as we talked, and he feared Sam would see us talking. I then congratulated him and told him I loved him. By then, my mom, Jeremy, and Rachel had caught up. We had enough time to take photos with Nick and arrange a time to have breakfast together the following day.

"We picked Nick up at 8:00 am and headed to breakfast. Jeremy and Rachel were so excited to spend time with their big brother. Most of the conversation centered around those three, and I sat back and enjoyed the interaction. Nick was not ready to return home after everyone had breakfast, but I went ahead and paid the check.

"My mom suggested we go bowling as she and my sister had several hours before they needed to be at the airport. I cannot tell you the last time I had bowled before that day. We arrived at the bowling alley, got our shoes and balls, and began playing. As everyone was taking turns, Nick started revealing various incidents in the past few years. The first one entailed an auto accident he was in where he swerved and veered off the road into a ditch. Fortunately, Nick was not injured, and no other cars were involved. I asked him where his dad in all this was. His response was, 'Out of town.' I then asked him how he got home, to which he said the police took him back home. I pressed further and inquired if the police asked where his parents were. He replied that he did tell him of the divorce, that his dad had custody, and he was out of town for the week. I was shocked that nobody ever told me, and the police were okay with a teenager being at home alone. I remember my mom and I stared at each other in disbelief."

Martha stopped talking when she saw Amy coming toward Liz. "Mom, did you bring some water?"

Liz pulled out the water bottle from her bag and handed it to Amy. She took a couple of sips, wiped the sweat off her brow, took a couple more drinks, and handed the water bottle back to Liz. Amy headed back towards Jess and Sydney.

Martha continued her story, "We each took a few more turns at bowling, making sure we kept the mood light for Jeremy and Rachel. I was trying hard for them not to notice any negative vibes. About thirty minutes later, Nick informed us that Sam had to replace the door in his office. When I asked what happened to the door, Nick admitted that he pushed his dad into the door. I sat up straight in disbelief. I then asked him to tell me what had happened. 'Dad and I were arguing about something when he began to push me. He kept pushing me to egg me on, so I delivered one hard push, and he lost his balance, went into the door, and fell.' I was so shocked. I glanced at my mom, whose mouth was wide open in disbelief.

I told Nick that violence is not the way to solve issues. He agreed. Please know that at this time, Nick was four to five inches taller and about fifty pounds heavier than his dad. Therefore, Nick was in the position of doing some physical harm."

Liz interrupts, "Do you think Nick was reacting to the beating he received as a child?"

"That thought crossed my mind," Martha replied. "Several years before his graduation, something happened, and I remember asking him about the beating incident. Nick didn't recall it, and I figured he blocked it out of his memory. But after he told me about this incident, I questioned if his reaction was due to the blocked memory. Unfortunately, that is something I will never know."

Martha and Liz sat quietly, watching their kids play. Liz reached over and held Martha's hand as a gesture of support. Martha smiled and continued, "Before you know it, it was time to take Nick back to his home and my mom and sister to the airport. When we stopped in front of Nick's home, I told him I hoped Sam wouldn't be too upset as we kept Nick out longer than anticipated. Nick said he was sure he would hear about it. I peered at him and said, 'You don't have to go back. You are always welcome with me.' As I was saying this, you could see that he was thinking about it, but after a minute said he would go in. He didn't want to deal with any aftermath that could arise.

"We hugged goodbye, and I headed for the airport. The drive to the airport was a quiet one. Tears were streaming down both my mom's and my face. I glanced in the rear-view mirror and observed my sister looking out the passenger side window, trying to hide her tears from Jeremy and Rachel. I hated seeing Nick in this situation but acknowledged he wasn't ready to walk away as I had. I kept praying for him."

"How is your relationship with Nick today?" Liz asked.

"It's great now, but it took a long time to get to this point. For many years, he was very distant, especially after I moved to California. I speculated he believed that I abandoned him when I moved, but he was eighteen and of legal age by that time. Those were tough years. I did call him once a month to say hello and ask how he was. The conversations were brief as he found excuses not to talk. I didn't see him for many years either. However, as time passed and I stayed consistent with checking in, he finally came around and re-established our relationship. It was quite a surprise when Nick told me, ' I now understand why you made the decisions you did.' While I never expected to hear words like this, I felt vindicated and, most importantly, forgiven."

Martha looked at Liz for her reaction.

Liz told her, "That's an incredible turnaround in your relationship. What is Nick doing now? Is he married? Have kids?"

Martha chuckled from the bombardment of questions and answered, "Nick is still living back east, where he has a wonderful job. He has never married and has no kids. I still have hope that he will find the right person."

"I have to hand it to you, Martha; I've never seen anyone exude as much hope as you do," said Liz.

"My faith in God gives me this hope. I don't know any other way to live. I love Romans 12:12, which says, 'Rejoice in hope, endure in affliction, persevere in prayer.'[5] This passage sums it up for me."

Liz smiled.

Jess ran up crying. Another little boy was taking over the slide and not letting others take turns. Liz listened to Jess intently as he was telling her this, and then he asked to go home. Liz got Amy, and the three of them left.

Martha stayed a bit longer, watching Sydney have fun going down the

5   Holy Bible, The New American Bible, World Publishing, 1970

slide. They soon leave the park for the day.

The organized chaos of the afternoon would begin in a couple of hours, with the bus dropping off Sarah and Michael, homework getting started, and dinner being prepared. Martha smiled. She was content with her life and knew she was right where she needed to be. Life was good!

CHAPTER 21

FAMILY HEALING

Over the next few days, Martha took Sydney to the park, but Liz, Jess, and Amy did not show up. Getting concerned, Martha texted Liz to see if all was well. She did not respond. Sydney kept asking where Jess and Amy were. Martha told her the truth, which was, she didn't know. As Sydney played, Martha said a prayer for Liz and her family and then turned to read her book, periodically looking up to check on Sydney. Martha tried to concentrate on reading her book, but her reflections kept drifting to Liz. Before long, it was time to take Sydney home.

Martha made Sydney a peanut butter and jelly sandwich for lunch. While Sydney ate her lunch, Martha's phone pinged, indicating she had received a text message. The message was from Liz, who thanked her for her concern but said all was well and they would be back at the park tomorrow. Martha told Sydney the good news that her friends would be back tomorrow. Sydney grinned from ear to ear and then asked Martha to read her a story. Martha gladly complied with this request as it allowed her a chance to test Sydney on word recognition.

Sydney fell asleep while Martha was reading, and Martha carried her upstairs to her room. Then Martha turned her attention to the laundry and dinner preparation. The afternoon flew by, and it was soon time for dinner. At the dinner table, everyone took turns describing their day.

Sydney said, "I'm so happy that Jess and Amy will be back at the park tomorrow?"

Rachel asked, "Where have they been?"

Martha felt Rachel and James staring at her for this response. Not wanting to say too much in front of the kids, Martha volunteered that she didn't know and had texted Liz who indicated all was well, and they would be back tomorrow. James glanced down and shook his head in disbelief. Sarah and Michael took turns and talked about the school assembly they attended that afternoon. Rachel cleaned up the kitchen from dinner, and Martha went outside to sit on the front porch to watch the sunset.

After a few minutes, Rachel joined her and asked if Martha knows more than what she told at dinner. Martha assured her that she didn't know anymore and admitted being concerned. Both Martha and Rachel sat outside until the sun set over the mountains. Another day had come and gone, and it was time to prepare for tomorrow. Martha retreated to her room for the night.

The following day, Martha woke up hearing Michael's voice. She wasn't sure who he was talking to, but she got up and went downstairs to start breakfast. Soon everyone was up, ate breakfast, and then out the door. Sydney looked at Martha and asked, "Are you ready yet, Grandma, to go to the park?"

Martha chuckled and told her they would leave shortly. By 10:00 am, Martha and Sydney arrived at the park, but to their dismay, Liz and her kids were not there. Sydney frowned. Martha hugged Sydney and told her not to worry as they might be running late. Sydney was satisfied with this response and left to play on the jungle gym.

Five minutes later, Liz arrived with Jess and Amy. Sydney saw them and came running over to greet them. Liz and Martha hug. Once the kids were at the jungle gym, Martha asked Liz how she was doing.

She gave a curt response, "Fine."

Martha was a bit surprised at Liz's short answer, so trying to lighten the mood, she asked her how she was enjoying the new kitchen.

Again, Liz was blunt and said, "Fine."

Martha glanced away to watch the kids play.

"Martha," Liz began, "I have a question."

"Sure, what is it?" Martha replied. "How did Jeremy and Rachel handle the divorce? Were there any ramifications to them from your decision to leave Sam?"

Martha begins her response, "The short answer is yes. But each handled the divorce differently, and I attribute that to their sex and age when the divorce happened. As soon as I moved to California, I found a family therapist, Dr. Grant, and solicited her help so we would truly begin the process of healing. Jeremy was still exhibiting anger issues, which manifested in punching holes in the wall, and I was genuinely concerned that he would be following in his father's footsteps. Dr. Grant performed a battery of tests on Jeremy and Rachel. She indicated that Jeremy was exhibiting a depression disorder and prescribed medication. Rachel was very clingy to me, and the testing confirmed it. The real icing on the cake for me was when Dr. Grant stated that she needed to get Sam involved in the healing process. I told her she was crazy for suggesting this and asked if she had listened to anything I said about the history of abuse we all endured. I asked her why I would subject my children to this again. I was livid and walked out.

"After praying about this and speaking with my parents, I returned to Dr. Grant. The consensus from my family is that she must see Sam's manipulation in action to see the true picture. Arranging this was difficult as Sam's interaction with the kids was limited. In the meantime, the medication was helping Jeremy as his anger had tapered down."

"You must have sensed that you were going backward," Liz interjected.

"I sure did, and I was extremely frustrated. My goal was to get these kids healthy mentally, and it wasn't happening. The therapy sessions continued for a few months until Sam decided to come to town unannounced. Sam and his wife went to Dr. Grant's office and demanded an explanation of Jeremy's medical condition. You see, per the divorce decree, Sam was responsible for paying for the medical and dental insurance until they were of age. So, he was getting copies of the charges, which he has every legal right to see. However, I didn't expect him to go into the doctor's office unannounced. About an hour after this incident, Dr. Grant called me and told me what had happened. She went on to say a few more words, most of which I can't repeat but suffice it to say that she was now in my corner. From her brief encounter with Sam, she diagnosed him as a narcissist. I now had her commitment to helping me get these kids healthy emotionally. What a relief."

"How did they do in school? Any issues?" Liz asked.

"Rachel didn't have any issues with school, but Jeremy, on the other hand, was a different story. Jeremy never liked school from day one. Over the years, his dislike of school became worse. He would skip classes and school altogether. Around the time he was fifteen or sixteen, it was all I was able to do to encourage him to pass his classes. His anger issues manifested again, and Dr. Grant changed the medication, hoping it would help. I later learned that he was not taking those meds but was self-medicating with illegal substances. I was devastated. With Dr. Grant's help, Jeremy went to a rehab facility for several weeks.

"When it was time to come home, he was clean, and things were good for a while, but he slipped up again. This time, Jeremy was failing in his senior year of high school. The school called me and was discharging him as there was no way he would pass and graduate. I went to the school and picked up the needed paperwork, and as I left the school to drive home, tears came streaming down my face. I believed that I had failed Jeremy between failing school and his drug use. I now know that these were his choices, and he had to pay the consequences, but as a mother, I wanted to protect him from these mistakes. I entered Jeremy into another rehab facility, where he stayed for a couple of months. Again, when he came home, he was clean, and life was good. When it happened a third time, I told him enough was enough. He had just turned eighteen, and I told him he had to leave. I was not going to put up with this any longer, and since he was of legal age, my job now was to protect Rachel from seeing all of this. His friend, who was also using drugs, picked him up that night. They moved into an apartment near where I lived. Kicking him out of the house was the hardest thing ever."

Martha stopped speaking and reached for her bottle of water. Amy came running up to Liz, asking for some water and was soon followed by Sydney asking for the same. After a few minutes, the girls went back to play.

Turning to Martha, Liz asked, "Where was Sam in all this? Did he know what was going on with Jeremy?"

"Yes, he did," Martha replied. "He responded that it was my problem and told me I was a bad mother. I hung up the phone on him. I knew better! At any rate, a couple of months after I kicked Jeremy out of our home, I got a call from the Sheriff's Department. The call came in around 11:00 pm, and the Sheriff asked that I come down to the station. Rachel and I went to the station only to learn that Jeremy and his roommate, robbed at gunpoint inside their apartment., were being detained at the Sheriff's Department. The Sheriff suspected a drug deal going down went bad. It was evident by Jeremy's behavior that he was high. I provided the Sheriff with a condensed version of my life and made sure the Sheriff comprehended that Jeremy had been in rehab not once but twice and removed from the home. I asked him if there was any way he could lock up Jeremy for the night to 'scare him' into getting clean. The Sheriff informed me that the law had changed and now prohibited this. He understood what I was doing and was disappointed he couldn't be more help. It was 2:00 am. With Jeremy having nowhere to go, I told him he could come home for the night but that I was taking him to a halfway house first thing in the morning as he would not stay with me in his condition. He said he understood."

The two women sat quietly on the bench for a couple of minutes, watching the kids play and intermittently taking sips of water.

Liz quietly asked, "Martha, I'm afraid to find out what happened next."

Martha smiled, and beaming, said, "This one has a great ending."

Liz perked up and responded, "Please tell me!"

Still smiling, Martha continued, "The next morning, I grabbed the keys to take Jeremy to the halfway house. I glanced towards the patio, and he was sitting there crying. I was stunned but secretly hoped that he had finally hit rock bottom. Praying to God that this was the sign I had been hoping for, I was afraid as I didn't know if I could trust him. As I opened the patio door, I saw Jeremy crying gut-wrenching sobs. I had never seen him in this state before and asked him what was wrong as I sat down. He responded, 'All this time, I have been angry with you, but I really should have been angry with dad.' I told him that I knew that. He stared at me, surprised by my answer, but he saw the look of unconditional love I had for him, and I saw his heart melt. I told Jeremy that his dad did not want us to succeed and that he needed to get even rather than get angry. I reminded him that even Jesus got angry, and being angry is a valid emotion, but what we do with our anger can cause us to sin, which we need to avoid. You can get even by making something of yourself. Use the anger and channel it in the right way to better yourself. Jeremy took this to heart as he tried to enlist in the U.S. Army but to do so, he needed a high school diploma. Jeremy went to the local junior college, earned his diploma, and enlisted in the Army. He spent several weeks in boot camp back east. When the time came for him to graduate boot camp, I flew out there and watched him march with immense pride. It provided me great pleasure to have the honor of pinning the blue cord around his arm sleeve. A few months later, he deployed to Afghanistan for a year fighting in that war. Fortunately, he returned home unharmed. Now he has a wonderful job, a home, a wife, two kids, and is happy."

"Oh my gosh, Martha! What a remarkable story! I just got goosebumps," Liz exclaimed.

"But how did you deal with all that stress during that time?" asked Liz.

"It wasn't easy," Martha claimed. "There were many nights I cried myself to sleep, begging God to intervene and help Jeremy. I did not want to deal with having to bury a child as I was afraid that would do me in. At that time, I found Psalm 46:10, 'Be still and know that I am God.'[6] One day, in the middle of all this chaos with Jeremy, I was driving and observed this huge billboard with the words 'Be Still.' I had been praying for direction on what to do with this situation, and He answered me. God was working on this, and He wanted me to be still and wait on Him. And boy, did He ever! There have been other times when things were going on, and I put it in prayer, asking for help in resolving the issue. Sometimes I am unsure if it is something I need to resolve or if He is working on it. When I see, hear, or read the words 'Be Still,' I know He is working on it. What is hard for me is to have the patience to wait. I am the first to admit that I am a continual work in progress."

Liz started laughing, and Martha joined her. It was great to laugh, and Martha would see that laughter was a fantastic way for Liz to release whatever she was holding in.

Martha commented, "It seems like you are in better spirits."

6   The Holy Bible, Revised Standard Version Catholic Edition, Oxford University Press, 2004

Liz replied that she had a lot on her mind. She then asks about Rachel and the impact of the divorce on her.

Martha answered, "Rachel was only four when the divorce became final. She did well in school, and the only issue I saw was her tendency to be clingy with me. She was too clingy and didn't want me out of her sight. As time went on, the clinginess dissipated, which is a good thing. She went on to get a bachelor's degree and a master's degree in music. Rachel has a beautiful voice, and when she sings 'Ave Maria,' the tears come to my eyes. From time to time, Monsignor will request that she perform it at church. Rachel is married now, as you know, with three kids of her own."

"What about any contact or relationship with Sam? Do they ever talk to him?' Liz inquired.

"The short answer is no," Martha responds. "Once I moved to California, the visits became less and less. Sam and his wife would make an annual trip to California but only spend one or two days with the kids while they spent the rest doing who knows what. Sam would show up unannounced demanding to see the kids. He would typically go to their school to see them, but since he was not listed as a contact because I did not have his contact information, the school would not release the kids to him.

"On one occasion, the school called me directly as he showed up, and when the teacher told Rachel that Sam was there to see her, she turned white as a ghost from fear. The school called me and told me what had happened. They were very concerned for Rachel, and I advised the school I would come to pick her up. Sam called me upset about what happened at the school. I informed him that I was totally unaware of his visit. I reminded him of the custodial agreement. He demanded to see the kids, so I arranged to meet at a local grocery store parking lot. This was for the safety of the kids and myself as I figured there would be people around in a parking lot to be witnesses should they be needed, to any outbursts.

"While I was dropping off the kids in the grocery store parking lot, Sam came up to my car and started banging on the windows with his fists and yelling profanity. The window pounding was so intense that I feared the window would break, so I picked up my phone to call the police. He left before the police came. However, I filed a restraining order as I feared for my safety as well as the safety of my kids. While I know restraining orders are only as good as the paper they are printed on, I wanted a record on file just in case anything ever happened."

"Did Sam try to do anything else to harm you?"

Martha looked at Liz and nodded affirmatively. Martha continued, "Sam took every opportunity he could to throw me a curve ball when it came to custody of the kids. One time, he reported me to Child Protective Services for no apparent reason. What was surprising to me was that it took several months for someone from this agency to contact me. When they finally reached out, a representative arranged a time to inspect my home. She asked me a few questions and then left. After that, there was no other communication from the agency."

Liz gave Martha a puzzled look and said, "Wow, that is very strange."

"I agree," Martha responded and then continued, "I knew the kids were in the best possible situation with me, but I did question the caseload these workers had and pitied the children who needed help but were unable to receive it. So, on the one hand, it bothered me I didn't get a response. On the other hand, however, I was glad that there was no further communication with Child Protective Services."

Martha paused to drink some water. Liz asked her if there were other incidents.

Martha responded, "Yes, there was one more I can recall, and I found it amusing." "What was that?" Liz inquired. Smiling.

Martha recounts the incident where Sam had written a letter to one of the Dioceses telling them that I am a bad Catholic, unfit mother, and the church should do something about it.”

“What? How did you find out about it?” Liz exclaimed.

Now chuckling, Martha said, “The funny thing about the letter was that Sam wrote to the wrong Diocese. The Diocese copied me on the response to Sam, and the Diocese told Sam that it was a legal issue, not a church issue. In other words, go pound sand.”

Liz understood how low Sam stooped and shook her head in disbelief. “Anything else? I’m afraid to ask?”

Martha replied, “No, that’s about it. Communication ceased once Sam stopped paying child support when Rachel came of age. It’s too bad because he missed out on so many milestones.”

Martha paused and drank some water. She saw Liz reflecting profoundly and said, “Everything okay?”

Liz smiled. “Yes, I am okay. Your story is one of hope, especially for single-parent households. I don’t know if I could have done what you did.”

“Liz,” Martha said, “No one knows what challenges and blessings lie ahead. My goal was to provide a healthy, loving environment for my kids. In this case, I had to do it alone without their father. But I wasn’t alone. Long ago, I learned to rely on God as my compass. He continues to keep me focused and on the right path. Find your compass, Liz. For me, my compass is God.”

Liz glanced at her watch and said she had to go home. She called out for Amy and Jess. Liz embraced Martha and thanked her for sharing her story. As they hugged, Martha got a funny feeling that something wasn’t right.

Liz and the kids left, and soon Sydney ran to Martha and said she is ready to go home. They left the park.

Martha tried to shake the ominous feeling she got when hugging Liz. She hoped that Liz was okay and said a quick prayer for her. Martha opted to bake chocolate chip cookies to distract her mind, and Sydney was right there to lick the bowl. The rest of the afternoon proceeded as usual; soon, everyone was at the table to eat dinner.

When it was Sydney's turn to talk about her day, she told everyone that she saw Amy and Jess. Martha was quiet and continued eating. As Sydney spoke, she perceived that Rachel was looking at her for a reaction. Martha remained quiet. After dinner, Martha went to the family room to join the others in watching television. Rachel asked Martha if she was okay. Martha told her about the feeling she got when hugging Liz and that she couldn't seem to shrug it off. Rachel asked her for more details.

Martha replied, "I can't describe it other than to say that I feel like something bad is going to happen." Rachel hugged Martha and told her everything was okay. Martha retreated to her room for the night.

CHAPTER 22

A TIME FOR MOM

Martha awakened to her cell phone ringing. She quickly looked at the time and saw that it is 2:20 am. 'Who would be calling at this hour?' Martha wondered. She picked up her phone and saw Liz's name and a number on the caller I.D.

Groggily, Martha answered, "Hello."

"Martha, I am so sorry to have wakened you," spouts a frantic Liz.

"It's okay, Liz; what is going on?" Martha asked.

Liz started crying, "Martha, I am at the hospital. Jeff and I got into an awful fight, and he hit me."

"What?" Martha exclaimed. "Let me get some clothes on, and I will be right there,"

Martha quickly dressed and woke Rachel to tell her what happened and where she was going. She then took off to the hospital.

Arriving at the Emergency Room, Martha entered and headed to the nurse's station. She inquired about Liz with the head nurse, who told her to wait in the lobby. A few minutes later, the nurse called Martha's name and took her behind the doors to see Liz. Arriving at Liz's area, the pulled-back curtain revealed a very battered-looking woman.

It was Liz, but Martha hardly recognized her. With her right eye almost swollen shut, evidence of facial bruising appeared. Dried-up blood remained on her lip, which had been split open.

Martha observed that Liz was holding her right arm. "What's wrong with your arm?" Martha asked.

"The doctor is checking for broken bones. I am waiting for the results of the x-ray."

Martha shook her head in disbelief and sighed. "Liz, who is watching the kids? Where's Jeff?"

Liz told her that Amy and Jess were with a neighbor, and the police arrested Jeff. "You called the police?" Martha inquired.

"Yes," Liz replied with her eyes looking downward.

"Good," Martha replied emphatically.

Their conversation was interrupted by the doctor who had just come in. He told Liz that her arm had a hairline crack and would need a cast. Liz just stared at the doctor as he told her these words, but she did not respond. Finally, the doctor left, and tears began streaming down Liz's face. The salt from her tears hit the open wounds on her lip, and she flinched. Martha placed her hand on Liz's back and assured her everything would be okay. A nurse entered the area with the materials needed to put the cast on Liz's arm. Martha told her she would wait outside in the lobby.

Martha found a comfortable chair in the lobby to sit in and picked up a magazine to read. As she glanced around, she saw only one other person in the room at this hour. 'Must be a quiet night for the ER,' Martha observed.

She began to read the magazine but realized she couldn't focus on the words. Instead, her mind drifted and she wondered how she could have been of more help to Liz. 'Liz didn't deserve what happened to her. And, what about the kids? They must be so worried about their mom. What are they thinking about what their dad did?'

Martha began to sense her blood pressure rising as these thoughts raced through her mind. She took some long, deep breaths to calm down.

The doors to the patient area suddenly opened and out came Liz with her arm in a blue cast. She walked over to Martha.

"Let's get you home," Martha said.

When they arrived at Liz's house, Amy and Jess saw their mom and gave her big hugs. The looks of relief at seeing their mom walk through the door was evident on their little faces. Martha made sure that Liz got in and settled before leaving. She told Liz that she would check in on her in a few hours but not to hesitate to call anytime. Liz thanked Martha for her help.

When Martha arrived home, she was warmly greeted by her grandkids, each asking where she had been. Glancing at Rachel, she told them she was helping a friend. Rachel told Martha that she had things under control for the morning routine and suggested Martha go upstairs to get some rest. Martha laid down on her bed but could not fall back asleep. She kept reliving Liz's battered face in her mind, and it pained her that Liz had to deal with that.

Knock! Knock! Martha's door opened and it was Rachel who let her know that Sarah and Michael had left for school, and she was off to work. Sydney came rushing in and jumped on Martha's bed. She reached out to hug her, and Sydney got under the covers to snuggle with her. Martha told Rachel goodbye and to have a wonderful day.

Martha turned to Sydney, "Grandma is tired today. I think we will take it easy and watch some movies."

Sydney smiled and replied, "Okay, Grandma. Can we make some chocolate chip cookies today, too?"

"Sounds like a good plan, Syd," Martha responded. She got up, made her bed, and got cleaned up. She found Sydney occupying herself by having a tea party with her dolls. Martha asked to join in and watched Sydney's creative conversations, over tea, with her dolls. Soon after, the tea party was over, and it was movie time, followed by some baking in the kitchen. Yet Martha kept Liz on her mind and hoped she was doing well under the circumstances.

The day flew by, Sarah and Michael arrived home from school, and everyone was at the dinner table talking about the day's events. After dinner, Martha went outside to sit on the porch. She texted Liz to check in to see how she was doing and if she needed anything.

Ten minutes later, Liz responded that she was okay.

Rachel and Sarah joined Martha on the porch to watch the sun disappear over the mountains. Sarah snuggled up to Martha, who could not help but say a quick prayer that God would always protect her grandkids from harm. Knowing what Martha was thinking about leaving her own abusive marriage, her suicide attempt, and years of rebuilding her life, Rachel reached out and held Martha's hand. She understood her mom all too well!

Martha was the first up the following day and went downstairs to fix breakfast. Soon she was joined by the other family members, who quickly ate breakfast and rushed off to school or work, leaving Sydney and her. Martha took Sydney to the park but did not expect to see Liz and her kids because she recognized Liz had a lot on her plate.

As Sydney was playing, Martha texted Liz to see how she was. Liz responded, thanked her for her concern, and mentioned she was speaking with attorneys.

"'Well, that's good news," Martha muttered. Sydney ran towards Martha and got her water bottle out of her bag. She did announce that Amy and Jess were not there and asked Martha if she knew where they might be.

Martha responded, "No, Sydney, I don't know where they are. It looks like it is just you and me today."

Sydney returned to the jungle gym. It was just Martha and Sydney at the park for the next several days. Neither Martha nor Sydney saw Liz, Amy, or Jess. Martha stayed connected with Liz, who said she was healing up nicely.

A week passed, and Martha and Sydney were surprised to see Liz, Jess, and Amy on the daily trip to the park. Sydney ran ahead of Martha and hugged Amy and Jess. Then, they ran off to the jungle gym. Martha made eye contact with Liz, who smiled. The two women embraced with a warm, heartfelt hug.

Martha had been concerned about Liz and was relieved that she was back. The bruises on Liz's face were almost gone, and her lip had healed with the swelling gone. They sat on the beige wooden bench, and Martha asked Liz about her arm.

"It's healing nicely," Liz responded.

"That's so good to hear! How is everything going, Liz?" Martha inquired.

Liz thanked her for the concern and told her she appreciated her texts. During her absence from the park, Liz told Martha that she hired an attorney, filed for a divorce, and filed a restraining order against Jeff.

Jeff had committed to attend counseling to deal with his anger issues, but Liz was not sure if he would honor the commitment. She also told Martha that she was moving closer to her family as they had committed to helping her raise the kids.

"You're really going to move?" Martha asked.

"Yes, it will be better for the kids and me to have more support," Liz replied.

"I understand and honestly would make the same decision. It is important to have the support and love of family, but I will certainly miss you,"

Liz smiled.

"Martha," Liz began, "do you mind if I ask you some more questions?"

"Sure," Martha replied, "what do you want to know?"

Liz began, "You have been so open about the struggles with your kids and the abuse in your marriage. What I would like to know is what did you learn along the way? And how do you deal with loneliness?"

"Wow," Martha responded, "those are serious questions. Let me think about the best way to answer them."

Just as Martha was going to reply, Jess came up and asked for water. He took a few sips and hugged Liz before returning to play with Amy and Sydney. Liz apologized for the interruption.

"The best way to answer this is to use the last words that Sam told me and begin there. If you recall, he told me, 'You will never make it, and no one will ever love you.' Well, I did make it. When I separated from Sam, I was a stay-at-home mom. Computers and the internet were just coming into existence, and cell phones did not exist. I had basic administrative skills but no computer skills. I was hired as an office manager and taught myself basic programs, like MS Word and Excel, to get up to speed. After relocating to California, I found work at a property management firm that specialized in managing homeowners' associations. Although hired as their office manager, a community manager submitted his notice three months later, so I went to my boss and said I wanted to do that job. He told me to 'have at it,' and I spent the next twenty-plus years in the industry.

"I managed several types of communities: condominiums, townhomes, mobile homes, high rises, and single-family homes. I worked both as a portfolio manager and an on-site manager and eventually became a supervisor. I had no knowledge about the industry, so I took courses and attended various educational trainings as my schedule permitted me to.

"I earned a state designation and the highest national designation in this industry. In addition, I returned to school and earned a Bachelor of Science Degree in Organizational Leadership. I took every opportunity to learn my trade and move up the proverbial ladder. I provided a modest lifestyle for myself and my kids through the years, including retiring comfortably enough to travel. I proved that I didn't need him to succeed as I already had what it took. All I needed was the confidence in myself to achieve these accomplishments."

Liz's eyes opened in amazement as Martha shared this. "Martha, you certainly did well for yourself, and this gives me a lot of hope for my future.

"I'm glad to hear this, Liz," Martha replied and continued. "You have a lot to offer, so please don't settle or sell yourself short."

Liz smiled and perked up as if she suddenly recalled something to tell Martha. "Oh, guess what?" I forgot to tell you that I have a job lined up waiting for me to start as soon as I relocate."

Excited for Liz's future, Martha replied, "That's wonderful to hear, and I'm sure you will do well."

Liz and Martha took a break from talking to watch the kids play. Martha grabbed her water bottle and took a few sips.

"Martha," Liz said, breaking the silence, "aren't you lonely?"

Martha asked Liz if she was asking this question because she was afraid of feeling alone.

Liz stared at her.

"Liz, I am not alone, never have been. When Sam told me that no one would ever love me, I must admit those words stung. It felt like he stabbed me through my heart. For many years, I was so busy working on helping my kids that I didn't think about it too much. Yes, I struggled with loneliness but understood I wasn't alone because of prayer. However, Sam's words 'you will never be loved' have paralyzed me from time to time, and that is when I sought professional help. I've learned that the only kind of love that Sam could provide was not something I wanted, nor did I deserve. It's not love. Pure and simple."

"You are so right, Martha! That is not love," Liz said.

"Good, I am glad to hear you say this," Martha replied. "Truthfully, I began to seriously work on myself about fifteen years ago. Unfortunately, the years took their toll, and I acknowledged I was an emotional eater. I found myself extremely overweight, and when Rachel became engaged, I did something about it and lost over 100 pounds for her wedding. I wanted to wear this beautiful blue dress and worked hard to fit nicely in it. The wedding was a kick in the pants I needed to permit myself to focus on me. I figured that if I wanted God to provide the right person, I needed to be physically and mentally healthy. I am so glad I took this step, as I love enjoying my time with my grandkids. Between my kids, grandkids, and friends, I am so blessed and immensely loved. My heart is whole."

"But what about being lonely," Liz asked. "Have you considered remarrying?"

Martha smiled. "Yes, loneliness exists, and one can be in a crowded room and still feel lonely. It's about one's mindset. When those negative thoughts and feelings come over me, I work to rewire the negativity by praying and then remembering all of my blessings. It helps, and the negative thoughts go away. And, as far as remarrying? I am leaving that up to God. I would certainly consider it, but I need to find the right person. I am not expecting to find a perfect person, just a man that is perfect for me. There is a difference. I was in a relationship and have dated some, but nothing that would have led to marriage. Being Catholic, I was granted an annulment after going through an extensive and painful process of reliving my past. I wanted to be 'right' with God, so getting the annulment was another part of the healing process. I'm glad that I did this. I trust God. He has always provided and taken care of me. If remarriage is part of His plan for me, He will provide. I learned long ago to 'never say never' where God is concerned. He always has the last say and the last laugh!" Martha looks at Liz with her blue eyes twinkling, and both women burst into laughter.

Liz looked at her watch and indicated she needed to go. The movers were at the house and would be finished packing the household goods in the next hour.

Liz called for Amy and Jess, and Sydney returned with them. Liz told her kids it was time to go and to hug Sydney, which they gladly did. Sydney looked at Martha with a puzzled look. Martha explained that Amy and Jess are moving away, but there will be opportunities to call them.

As the children hugged, an older gentleman approached Liz and Martha. A blond-haired little girl, about four years old, was with him. Martha noticed that this distinguished, Cary Grant-looking man was about 6'3" with a slender build wearing black jeans and a royal blue polo shirt. His silver-gray hair highlighted his deep blue eyes, which stared directly at Martha.

"Excuse me, ladies! My name is David, and this is my granddaughter, Stephanie. We are new here in the neighborhood. Is it okay for Stephanie to play with your kids?"

David asked, smiling, and showing off his pearl white teeth.

Martha explained that Liz and her kids are about to leave but that she would be staying for a while longer.

"Great," David replied.

Martha bent to Sydney's level telling her to take Stephanie to the jungle gym area. Then she went to Liz, hugged her goodbye, and wished her well.

Liz glanced at Martha with a look that said, "Well, maybe this is the one?"

With a twinkle in her eyes, Martha looked back at Liz and said, "Remember, Liz, never say never."

THE END

RESOURCES FOR HELP

National Domestic Violence Hotline: 800-799-SAFE (7233)

National Alliance on Mental Health: 800-950-NAMI (6264)

Health Care Provider

National Institute of Mental Health: 866-615-6464

Local Court (restraining orders)

The Nicole Sinkule Foundation: https://www.nicolesinkule.org/

WORKS CITED

"*Gaslighting,*" Merriam-Webster Dictionary, Merriam-Webster, www.merriam-webster.com/dictionary/gaslighting. Accessed 13 June 2022.

"*How to Tell If Someone Is Gaslighting You,*" Newport Institute, https://www.newportinstitute.com/resources/mental-health/what_is_gaslighting_abuse. Accessed 13 June 2022.

Holy Bible, The New American Bible, World Publishing, 1970.

"*#TakeAStand Against Domestic Violence,*" Centers for Disease Control and Prevention, https://www.cdc.gov/injury/features/intimate-partner-violence. Accessed 21 June 2022.

The Holy Bible, Revised Standard Version Catholic Edition, Oxford University Press, , 2004

ABOUT THE AUTHOR

Debbie Griffiths was born and raised in the greater Los Angeles area. She graduated with honors from Biola University with a Bachelor of Science degree in Organizational Leadership. This degree helped her advance in the homeowners association industry, where she has written several articles on common interest developments.

Always trying to broaden her horizons, Debbie chose to write her first novel revolving around the trauma inflicted by gaslighting. This novel is a fictionalized story of a woman's quest to successfully rebuild her life with grace and courage following a painful divorce where she was a victim of domestic abuse.

As a result of this novel, Debbie created Broken to Boldness LLC as an avenue to bring more awareness to domestic abuse. The company's website, www.brokentoboldness.com, is a source for education and resources to help educate on recognizing the red flags of abuse and provide avenues to empower those wanting to safely leave these relationships.

Debbie is the proud mother of three grown children and considers her faith and family most important. She enjoys reading, needlework, genealogy, and playing golf in her spare time.